Road
to the Stilt House

David Adams Richards

ISBN 0 88750 574 0 (hardcover)
ISBN 0 88750 575 9 (softcover)

Cover art by David McKay. Book design by Michael
Macklem.

Printed in Canada

PUBLISHED IN CANADA BY OBERON PRESS

For Peggy, as always. And for Bill Bauer, old pal.

Part One

Man can overcome any fate by scorn—Albert Camus.

For from henceforth there will be five in one house divided, three against two and two against three—Luke 12. 52.

Winter seemed to be drying out. Cold came and went each day. The hornets again took over the house.

In the left-hand corner of his room, beyond the window that stared out at the road, Arnold managed to poke at the hornets with a broom.

Another fight.

That's all life was about. If one thought of it enough. After supper this evening his girlfriend had left him again. He saw her walk across the road.

What was he to do?

He kept his courage. Courage that the social workers told him he must have to live—courage that the priest told him he should have to cope with living at close quarters, now that he'd come back from town.

He'd come back from town because he'd left his job at the theatre and there was nowhere else to go. It was the only job he'd ever had.

But now his mother was out of the hospital, and Randy was expected back. Though no-one was certain when he would come. On top of everything Mabel was in the same condition. She bent over and complained about her stomach much the same.

So fights weren't far away.

"You'll die in the hospital if you go back there," Sadie told her.

Arnold wanted to get even.

For were her operations necessary? He didn't understand anything about it.

They sat in the house, even on warm nights, hating anything each other said. The snow was black and hard in the fields but the world was a pad of dry earth, the roots of trees had broken the dry ground.

Ahhh.

So he kept his thoughts to himself.

Mabel was in a bad state all right. She said the operation hadn't done her any good, but she was afraid to go back to the doctor and tell him. It was her third operation.

"Why are you afraid?"

6

"Leave me alone."

"Why are you afraid—"

"Leave me alone—my stomach hurts."

She sat in her grey winter coat with her stockings rolled down about her ankles. The coat came down to her calves, and thread and lining brushed her legs. The coat still had a Christmas decoration on the lapel, as if she would be going to midnight mass.

She'd got the coat six years ago. Arnold once thought she'd looked pretty good in it, and she still wore it in the winter, though its life had been sucked out of it; and in the winter she put on a skittish pink scarf to dress it up.

"I'm afraid the doctor will blame me for not getting better," she said.

Arnold said nothing.

"I'm afraid to bother him all the time."

Tears came. She sniffed. Her coat pockets were filled with bingo markers, which jiggled when she made a move.

"I'm not the type of person who likes to have a lot of operations."

So there was nothing more to be said about it.

Arnold had a cold and went upstairs. His chest rattled when he breathed, and he was perverse enough not to bother breathing unless he had to. In the holes—made by black boots, made by nails, made by pictures that had long since disappeared—behind the wallpaper that was scarred and tragic, came the hornets like small-time dancers.

Sadie went back to her room.

Mabel sat on the couch smoking Export cigarettes.

Obviously May wasn't a good month, but other months were coming.

He sat on the edge of the bed and coughed, feeling a pain in his chest. A chest that was hairless except for the teats, hairless so that he was ashamed of his white ribs.

And the knife scar like a pink tail that ran across his belly.

May was a long month, one of the longest. So he hoped

his cold would get better. He hoped Mabel would put her winter coat away, for he was sad when he saw her wear it.

He hoped things would brighten up a little. There were no stars in the sky this evening, and the wind was still raw. His girl carried herself well when she walked in high boots across the black washed-out road and disappeared. How could he stop her?

Make a scene? Or get involved in a little bit of bloodletting?

When he covered up in bed he still smelled her. Yes, it was her and no-one else under the dirty sheets. He read the letter Randy had written them months ago from the foster home:

I love Mabel most it read. *Mostly I love Mabel, all the time, and then I love Arnold—and I hope to go to a movie and see him taking tickets, and after that I love Norman because he told me we are cousins, and then I love Sadie—and I've got her a present. And then I love Harry, who taught me pushups—but mostly Mabel!*

The letter had been passed back and forth so much, no-one bothered to read it anymore.

CHAPTER 1

Winter has gone.

Summer is coming.

And I suppose that's all anybody can hope for.

Today it started before I had even left the bed. Randy came home from the foster home, and he doesn't want trouble. But trouble followed us here and has remained.

Today will be another day. Someone spit in someone's face downstairs, though from the road, if anyone were to go by in their car and look at our house, which is raised on stilts and painted splashes of dirty red and green, they would think nothing wrong. You can hear almost nothing from the road unless it's a cold night, or a long raw evening.

I said prayers to my mother's hips, to her hard face, asking her to be quiet, asking her not to fight. Her voice distresses me most when I hear it first thing in the morning.

Perhaps someone is angry today because of the heat that crawls over their white stomachs, because of the dead facial hair in the sink, because of the plugged toilet straining to gurgle, because of the sweltering walls with its tragic wallpaper, its curious boats and children, its oversize holes made with boots.

"Seaweed," my mother said, "get up—"

"Arnold," Randy called to me, "I'm home—I'm here again!"

Heat rises off the road. It rises near us in the morning, so you can fry an egg on it, and settles like a vapour in the evening with the birds. It's a road in the back end of our province, tattooed and broken. They said they were going to make it larger, and there'd be a lot of commercial enterprise on it, and that it would be opened up to all sorts of things. They have even ploughed back some gravel a little—but they haven't done anything else. So the road looks like a grey snakeskin that follows the shale and ditches, and trees scared and fallen over.

I've gone outside to get away from the fighting, from the sound of confusion and anger. There's an old mattress-spring to sit upon here, to be alone for a while everyday. Randy's bicycle, new last autumn, has been left out all winter and is rusted away, with its plastic flags.

And here is the road that leads nowhere, save to "Our Church of the Gladdened Heart" and each day is the same, and each night too, the same, a pendulum swinging back and forth.

The fight will continue as long as possible so as long as I can I'll sit here. My mother and her boyfriend are at each other's throats today because her purse was stolen.

Now and then they rise up against each other, cursing and fighting. Who accuses who? One accuses the other but it doesn't matter.

Just like the Russians.

And sometimes friends of mine tell me things I don't want to hear. Last night at the Arcade someone, I don't know who, said:

"Jerry called your girlfriend a dirty bitch—you should get even."

"Yes," I said without thinking. "I'll get even—I'll get even first thing in the morning."

Often I try to take refuge, for there is always one matter or another.

My girlfriend Trenda tells me that my cousin Norman stole the purse, at our little circus, near the tent of human oddities.

She is quite definite it is Norman.

Sometimes there is nothing to do but to blame someone for something.

I wear a black hat with an orange feather in it—most of the feathers have fallen out though, so there is just the naked bone sticking up, like a bald finger into the night, and I wear red pants. Everyone in our family smells like dark winter, like the hide of a horse.

My father died when I was ten. After his death, and the drunken procession (that struck me as comical) to the graveyard with the little picket fence and all the flowers in blossom so that you smelled them with your tongue, things got no better.

I was taken to family court then, and saw a big building that had the odours of musty carpet and long cold stairways. I remember the November sun through the dark afternoon windows like blood. They were high windows, like those in a Catholic church but with no agonies upon them. The stenographer smiled at me from her corner. Just because of fights at my house, simple and direct without too much hitting.

And I went to school. When I was in school I slept in the heat, bed was never as warm. And a teacher threw a glass of water upon me while I slept and then denied it. So Norman, my best friend and cousin, cut her car tires with a broken bottle.

We waited for her after school. The snow fell soundlessly out of the sky, and was very pretty when it fell against the lights, though the road was snowed over and grey. She came out of the entranceway carrying books. And she was all alone.

"What are you going to do Norman?" I whispered. She looked like a very harsh old woman, though she may have been 35. Her hair was damp when the snowflakes touched it, and her lips were white.

I hid in the shadows behind the stone wall, and did my best not to say anything. When Norman came back we went home to supper, and nothing more was ever said to me about it.

So I quit school and worked taking tickets at the theatre. But now the theatre is a ghost, with all the memories in it. Though they still show movies, I don't work there anymore, for the seats are empty and broken, with the stuffing gone, and the aisles are dirty and silent. The exit sign had a bottle thrown through it last winter and now the walls have contracted and are chipped with cold. Grey spider webs cling to the corners and float in the air.

I know something about evening, about black moods and depressions though I don't know what to call them.

I was in town one winter, and stayed in an apartment with one light in the corridor. It was there I saw things that made my nerves bad.

One wall had a streak of dry brown blood that no-one had washed off, and the ceiling was filled with marks and dull with smoke. It was there where I got the name Seaweed when I went to take tickets at the theatre. I kept a kitten until the landlord said he was sick of fleas, and threw it outside, and the kitten, its back sticky with milk, meowed at the door all night long, and I lay awake hoping it would go away.

I had set up plastic flowers upon the table, and had a picture on the wall of a horse with red eyes. But the feeling in my head never has gone away, from then until now. How can it, when I don't know why it's there?

11

One day after a storm when I went outside I saw that the kitten was dead and its body was thrown into the garbage can to be hauled away like everything else. When I went to the landlord about it he looked at me as if I were crazy to make a fuss over it. And narrowed his eyes, and looked as if he wanted to spit at me.   Perhaps all of us are dirty, with black nails.

When I came back home I found that my mother had a new man in her life. I think that she has her own life to live. But assuming this is so, and days are days, which are endless, the fellow moved his own mother in, and has given her her own room. His name is Harry.

Today the baby birds are warm in the birdnests almost ready to fly. The man who has come here is watching me, from behind the dead curtain but what is that? We never know today what scrapes we'll be in before tomorrow. And anyway—all my days are the same.

There is a truck across the river and in the distance an American jet skims to the height of heaven, followed by its thunderous sound. A washbasin lies in the grass, blackened and wounded by 22 bullets, and there is a noise from the prison they are building here, a noise of machinery.

The earth smells of sulphur and urine.

The sky of sweet nothing. The heat is upon us.

And things have suddenly become silent in the house. As silent as a man ashamed.

Juliet has driven here to see how Randy is; Juliet, the social worker.

I sit on the cot-spring praying to my mother—praying to her dirty white arse, and the washbasin that has loosened its atoms in the heat, so I can smell it along with the spit from weeds. I listen like a criminal to the guilt seeping through the house boards, and crawling belly down across the hot porch.

Guilt at the edge of our trees.

Juliet has watched me through our dirty window, our smell of human sadness, has watched me for a moment. But that hasn't done anything to change my expression, an expression that Jerry told me is like cold lead on a cold evening—the lead as white as twilight in autumn.

What does it matter? My mother always has a different excuse to give for a fight. Today she says she has cramps. My feeling is one of wallpaper over my nose, the smell of hair blocking my thought and the stink of garbage in plastic bags, the rattle of flies trapped inside. Juliet looks my way again, as if to check upon me, and I blink.

I can remember it as far back as life itself. The blink to avoid the look of strangers in a room, the blink to look away from those who teased your mother about being dirty when you were ten; like the blink coming out of a movie, out of a theatre, in the middle of a scalding sun.

But each man must get along with himself. Father Billy has told us this. Each man must attempt to come to some truce with his own heart.

There is no more fight after a while. But perhaps it is for the best.

Everything is silent after a bit. We sit in silence waiting for evening, smelling the heat of midday, a smell not unlike tires they throw into the river after they'd burned them. The smell, not unlike pissing upon weeds and a thousand other things, not unlike dark houses on stilts. But to be fair, I believe I know nothing about it.

It is Randy's day home, and this is it. Another fight. A fist in the head of a homecoming. Yet no-one can make any excuse for it. No-one can make any excuse.

Juliet asked me last winter what I did, what I thought of local matters, what my interests were. I answered her as best I could.

I did nothing, I thought little of local matters and I had no interests. Then, thinking I'd spoken too much, I shut up. I haven't spoken to her since. I think she has dismissed anything I've had to say to her since then.

Now it's the circus' last day here, and there is someone yelling.

There is always someone yelling. Who can say what for? Youngsters yell to show off, or to frighten people. Men yell in anger, and you can hear the hatred for the life they lead. Women yell when they are drunk. That to me, is the most painful yelling of all.

Inside our house, there are three rooms downstairs, and everyone sits apart from each other. Harry wants my mother to go to the cops but Mabel has no idea who has taken her purse. Harry is sure that if she gives the story to the paper, people will come to her aid, and we'll get a lot of money—enough to do us. Harry's mother, Sadie, sits in the big chair by the television and argues with herself.

She is quite delighted to have had this happen to Mabel. She makes no bones about it.

Thinking of this I feel I should go to the police myself —or at least face Norman.

Our circus is the same every year—so why did she have to go there? This is my thinking. It has the same smell of sawdust, one trapeze artist in his yellow costume, the same; one bear, the toothless one with the tickbitten nose. The same tent of Human Oddities, with all the oddities sitting out on lawnchairs.

I first met my girl when I lived in town. She had been mixed up with drugs—though I don't make judgments. Perhaps I should have been on guard, but I only wanted to help her. So after I quit my job we went to our house.

Mabel said:

"I could just shit."

This made me embarrassed. Harry's mother, Sadie, said nothing. She smoked a cigarette and eyed the girl through a cloud of smoke. Trenda talked about being on her own since she was thirteen. To me she sounded as if she could rule the whole world. In the months that have passed through, between then and now, not once has it been easy going, and as yet there is no talk of marriage. She seems to invite gossip. Also, people tell me I run too many errands for her, like a slave. And buy her flowers that are left to die after we have sex in the bedroom.

But things happen here one day at a time, so I'm thinking everything will be better, and I won't be as sick of this summer as I was of last winter, with its growling fires of ice.

14

Last week, when we sat in the doctor's office, I could hear everything the doctor said. Did he know you could hear right through his walls?

The nurse stared at us as if she were not ashamed of this. And motioned to my mother to go inside. Mabel undressed in that room, and was examined. The doctor told her there is nothing wrong with her now except her diet and that she might try to keep clean.

The doctor told her to get dressed again, and Mabel came out, looking frightened. She put her sheet on the table and had to sign a form. The examination didn't last ten minutes.

Now she is upstairs complaining. But she is a fighter in her own right. She takes it in stride most of the time, I must admit. And I'm learning to more and more as I go along.

CHAPTER 2

Mabel wanted a garden but no-one wanted to help with it, and besides it was too warm.

From the radio came the song, which went:
"Your daddy don't know
What your momma's gonna do tonight."

And from inside his house, from inside the little windows with their yellow silk curtains, came a yellow light.

Harry didn't want to help much either. He went to town every evening there was a sex show on at the theatre. When he came home he sat brooding on the porch. Why don't you help—? Harry said. Why don't you? Arnold shot back. You've come back home to cause problems. Go to hell. And you have. Go to hell. Help with the garden.

It got no better, so Arnold refused to answer him.

This fight alone made him think the worst was about to

happen and he stared stubbornly at his gravel yard, a yard that sloped down toward the road, and rested on two colourless boulders, and a ditch.

Mabel worked alone. She bought seeds, and a book on how to plant them. But with two drills done a rain came that soaked the ground. They had to stay inside and when it dried, the soil, which was never any good, looked like yellow clay. Unopened bags of seed lay about the yard—a hoe lay here, a rake there, already rusting. It bothered Arnold to watch his mother bent over in the stubble alone, but his perversity remained.

"Arnold," she said, "when your father was alive we always had a garden—every year he was out in the back working at it."

He sat in the house.

It was his ambition to remove all such memories from his head.

"Arnold it's up to you—" Mabel would say.

"I think I'll watch TV."

They sat there a few warm nights. Then with no help to plant a garden, there was a fight. It happened in the kitchen one night when he went for a glass of milk. His mother cursed him for being lazy and told him to go away.

"Away—sure, where do you want me to go," he yelled.

Then since she could get no-one else to take an interest she sprinkled some sunflower seeds on a damp patch of earth.

Everyone felt guilty about not helping her and kept out of each other's sight.

So besides a few radishes, two giant sunflowers sprouted. They faced the house for two weeks in great strength and nobility. Then their heads fell off and rolled away, strewing their yellow and black pulp across the yard.

In the month of June, he played the video games in Johnson's barn. He was stuck in the black arcade with its bleating lights. Every morning, as long as he had a cent, he would go there, and he'd return home every night, miserable and angry if he had gambled money, spitting blood from his black teeth.

He stayed away from the woods and streams that surrounded him. He watched television instead. He dressed in a leather hat, and wore skintight pants.

This wasn't unusual for him or for anyone else, but he was teased about what he wore. He thought he might carry a knife, to get even with those who teased him, but then decided it would be no good to do that.

He sat at home and watched television instead. There was often a fight over this, for no sooner would he get interested in a program than Harry or Sadie would demand to watch something else.

They all threatened to kick the TV apart in front of one another's eyes, but he considered that it was only he who would have the guts to do this.

He threatened them about it, and then said nothing else.

It was hot this summer. The hottest. It made him suffer a lot. It made him lie in the dust, exhausted, by the riverbed. His girl and he, both three-quarters naked, let the sun crucify them. His girl displayed a remarkable passion for this. She lay with her body opened to the sun and talked to everyone. Under the passionate weeds, under the dark flat rocks, under the burning dust came one smell, like an ointment.

It was the smell of their own cesspool.

It made his head dizzy.

Other things made his head split.

His girl looked like a woman, in all aspects.

While Arnold's ribs showed.

One day he was walking up the white sewer pipe, while Jerry Bines was coming down toward the river.

They met near the middle of the pipe. It was a graduated climb and now they stood about eight feet above a dry gorge.

"How's your girl?"

"Good."

"Why don't you bring her with us some night—let her get a taste of a real man?"

Arnold laughed.

"Yes," Jerry said, smiling. "How could she be satisfied with you?"

Seaweed laughed again. Brown shale rocks jutted out in the heat.

"I must go Jerry," he said.

"A woman like that—needs me," Jerry said. Arnold felt angry, but he shrugged and moved on.

Jerry watched him.

"Coward," Jerry said.

He went home and lay down shivering. He had closed his bedroom door, and the wallpaper pressed on his heart more than ever—as if the wallpaper showing scenes of mundane and fruitless happiness was his accuser. Downstairs Mabel was talking and yelling at Randy, who had done something with the potato masher. His bedroom smelled of dirty underwear and the slick that comes off washtaps.

"What does one do," he thought, "if he does not carry a knife in his pocket?"

The wallpaper, the smell of raspberries on wild bushes outside that rose with the dust and heat of their road, mingled oppressively in his heart.

"What stupidity," he considered, "to worry."

However, the closer he watched Trenda the more she seemed to change. She no longer talked to him so they quarrelled and avoided each other. Some days she went to the beach alone and stayed out all night. Sometimes no-one would go near him. Because of the look on his face.

He would lie awake at night, and he would try to think things over.

Jerry now openly ignored him.

He tried to laugh at it. But the same black feeling as there had been in the apartment, and even earlier than that, came over him.

"Ah well," he thought, "it'll all come out in the wash."

18

Except, he knew, no-one washed, in his house.
(This was the time the sunflowers rose and faced the house. They had a beauty that was unflinching. They could look him right in the eye, and say "—is it you who planted me—?" He, living as he was, felt that the creation was quite a bit more beautiful than its creator. His mother was pleased with them. She too could be caught staring at them, and smiling, as if they were better than anything else she had seen in the yard.

"If Jerry says anything more to me—I will carry a knife," Seaweed thought, looking at them.)

There was nothing to say on behalf of the yard, because nothing grew there. A little yellow grass maybe. Strangleweed, and near the road, long banana-shaped stinkweed.

There was nothing in the yard to mark it from other yards along the black fierce road. Of course there were better yards—to his thinking all yards were better than his own. The idea of "there's no place like home" was not in his soul. Matheson's yard had a small pond in the back, and a green swing for the children. The fat bees made noises there all summer long.

To say that people came into the yard and were friendly and happy was not the case. For instance, cards were played everywhere else. But there were no games played at his house very often. Others had nothing to do with them. Until he was older he didn't realize that people had card games in the evenings and a lunch afterwards. In his house in the winter the smell of oil soaked the kitchen. And it must be said that after the oil stove went out, the dark cold took over, with its unearthly smell.

In the winter it was a great land filled with sunset fires. In the summer it was a pad of dry earth.

A short distance from his house was a sewer pipe, which the provincial government built in a great hurry, and then blocked off. So it was never put to use.

Everyone laughed about it.

A government inspector came with two land surveyors; looked at the river, the sewer pipe, the road and the houses and then went away.

Everyone made fun of him.

So everything remained as it was.

Some nights the radio came on and he wanted to throw it against the wall.

And some nights the television punctured his ears.

With game shows, which told him how to win a lot of money.

And money was what they needed.

And sometimes his own house stank; so he could understand why Trenda stayed away.

"But what did she ever have," Sadie said.

"Be charitable," Mabel said.

Randy said nothing. He dipped some bread in molasses, and Harry scratched his lip.

"I can tell trash when I see it," Sadie said. "And I say what I see." She blew cigarette smoke away in little sad puffs, and then coughed up phlegm.

Too many nights Arnold shook and spit and couldn't look at anyone.

He waited to be called to go to work at the prison, and stared out the window. But the road told him things also. The prison wasn't hiring anyone—it merely reared its ugly head.

So everything remained as it was. Except one night an RCMP officer caught him coming from Johnson's Arcade with a knife.

"What's it for?"

"Nothing."

"Where are you going?"

"Nowhere."

"Can you tell me where you've been?"

"Playing Donkey-Kong."

"Ah yes," the officer said. He opened the blade of the knife and looked at it, was surprised at how deadly it looked. You could see he was surprised, and this made Seaweed content. He smiled. The officer noticed how sweet his smile was, a rather beautiful smile.

The officer asked him what he was going to do with it.

"Nothing—I've no use for it at all."

He'd been looking for Trenda all night—and he had thought if he saw her with anyone, he would use it. But he had not decided in any way, how he would use it.

"Then you don't mind if we keep it?"

"Not in the least—as I say, I've no use for it."

He had spent $15 on it. But he smiled throughout this ordeal, and the officer let him go along, minus the knife.

So everything remained as it was. The heat, the flies rattling under plastic bags, the dirty wallpaper in upstairs rooms—all remained as they were.

Trenda's eyes avoided his when he greeted her in the morning. And things were no better between her and the family.

"Where were you last night?"

"Nowhere."

"Did you have a good time?"

"Not particularly."

"You must have, without me around."

"Don't be silly."

"Don't call me silly—I get enough of being called silly."

"Well don't act silly."

"Who's acting silly?"

His face often turned leaden, like an evening in November with the leaves rotted, and the trees as bare as black whips. And things were no better for his brother.

Arnold awoke to the misery every day. What had Randy done? Peed on the toilet seat, or left dirty underwear behind the stove? Tracked sand into an already dirty house through a morning-cold kitchen? Any one of these. But Sadie had him by the hair and was making him scream.

Arnold came to the bottom of the stairs and shivered in the cold morning light. She had backed Randy up against the sink, and choosing a glass with the utmost care filled it to the brim with filthy dishwater.

And when she hauled his sandy hair he drank all right. As much as she could force down him.

As much as his stomach could hold.

But, be that as it may, Seaweed was no good at stopping it.

"Look!" he said. "Isn't that enough? He'll begin to bloat up."

He scratched his red hair until it came out in his hand, and itched his scalp until there was blood on his fingers.

In the afternoon the heads fell off the sunflowers and rolled away toward the boulders at the bottom of the hill. Randy was sitting on the porch with his fists clenched and Arnold went out to sit beside him.

"When I get big—no-one'll do that to me again."

They sat on the porch. It was mid-afternoon. A weed or two dragged its odour across the road and slept in the flat grey soil. The shadows made Randy look amphibian. His body looked like a lizard's. The cowlicks always stood up, the sun darted in and along his belly and shadowed the back of his neck to make it look scaley, and moved in and about his fingers to make them look webbed. His mouth was very small and his eyes were oval. He stared out at the world.

"She will never make you drink dirty water again," Arnold said.

He was determined that this be so.

And determination such as this he knew about. He put his arm about Randy and thought.

"She will never dunk him again."

This he vowed. Because he hated the woman, but he realized—determination such as this he saw in the eyes of boys before they broke down a doorway to steal money. Determination such as this he saw on the face of the social worker when she wanted to break up a bad family. Determination like this always made him aware of folly.

Yet—he was determined that this be so.

And why did he think this? He didn't know. Perhaps his heart wasn't hard enough to have such determination—like the determination Sadie had to choose the right glass from the cupboard, before she did her dirty work. It must be a glass that wouldn't break when Randy clamped his teeth against it—a glass that wouldn't cause a cut. She could get away with a lot, as long as she didn't cause bleeding. Such determination frightened him. But he let it go at that and tried not to think any more about it.

However Sadie herself made amends. She called Billy the priest, and had him come to the house so he could take the matter in hand.

"I'm an awful old woman," she said.

The priest asked Randy to go into her room, and to forgive Sadie.

"What lies," Arnold thought.

"Come now—have faith in God," the priest said. "All of you."

"It's lies," he said, loud enough for the priest to overhear him.

Later Sadie came downstairs to watch *Hawaii Five-O*.

The priest had gone on his way, after giving his blessing and blessing the house.

The priest said:

"Be forgiving to her—she is an old woman, and is losing her sight, she hasn't been to town to get her prescription filled. Remember, she has nothing now but memories."

All this the priest said. He knew the lecture was for him. He fidgeted and got angry. He got angry over the whole affair.

Sadie sat like an old elf in the broken rocker, watching *Hawaii Five-O*. She allowed Randy to have the big chair to curl up in, and told him a story about when she was a little girl, and how they carried torches in the winter from house to house, because there were no streetlights. She patted his hair and told a story of when Harry was a little boy. She told about the train ride they took and the number of towns they went through on their way, and where they were going and what they had packed in a basket. She tried to remember all the things they had for lunch that day.

Arnold told her to shut up.

23

So she stopped talking. Then she said:
"No-one's talking to me now—are they?"
And:
"I know who's jealous of me and who isn't in this house."
And:
"In this house—"
She started laughing to herself and saying:
'Oh yes, oh yes."
As if she knew something about them all.
—Whenever someone was hurt others would laugh.
—When Mabel lost at bingo they grinned from the corner.
—They all smelled like dirty wet cushions.
It was hard for Arnold to forget this.
Laughing to herself Sadie said:
"Arnold."
And then she would laugh, deeper, pronouncing his name in different ways, as if to figure out the best way to say it.
"Arnold."
He would hear her late at night.
"Arnold."
And then she would burst out laughing. It filled the hallway, and dragged itself throughout the black house.
It was a nuisance.
He'd listen to her, in the dark. He'd light a cigarette and the ashes would fall on his bare belly.
"There she goes—saying *Arnold* again," Randy would whisper to him.
"Go to sleep."

In the scorching heat there isn't a wave and you know that all these skins are going to burn and blister. But it is quiet.
It is strange to think of anything but the politics in my own house—the house on stilts.
My back is freckled and my hair is like red flame. I have a scar on my belly like a pink tail.

Everyone knows me here, so I'm nothing to them. We are—my family—all on welfare now. There are no unemployment stamps left at our house. When I wake in the morning I wait for the evening; in the evening I wish morning was here. Each day I play at the Arcade.

Then in the evening I eat like a pig, anything I can find. Potatoes, beans and wieners, macaroni—along with black tea—tea with seven teabags in a pot. Tea that's scorching and hot. There's always food, a lot if I want it.

My mother and I go out to town to see her doctor. After three operations there's nothing new about it. The doctor puts her up on the gurney and examines her pelvis, and puts his hand on her stomach. Each time she goes there she has hope. I don't think the doctor does anything for her—so why does she keep going back? The walls are brown and there are medical pamphlets everywhere. I've been here so many times I've counted the holes in the tile. Children cry in their mother's arms, and make annoying faces at my expense. When the children cry, at least we don't overhear the doctor telling my mother what is wrong with her insides. There's no privacy to an echo. When I hear him talking to her about herself—for instance that she is dry and sore, I turn my head away. When I chance to look up and see the young nurse glancing at me I try to make the best of it.

It is a basement office with a window that opens on a sordid parking-lot, with yellow dandelions in a rubbish-strewn field. You smell car metal in the heat. You think of the small town and the time you lived in it, the smell of the post office on your tongue. You try to remember the names of streets, and all the rest of it, the smell of the bakery at four o'clock on Christmas eve when it was snowing and you went to buy hot rolls. This takes your mind from other things, from the pens and pencils, the welfare form your mother signs. The doctor is a young man, hardly ten years older than myself. When he looks at me, as he did yesterday afternoon, for a second, it's as if he is from a different age. My hat always gives me away.

When we went home last night the politics at my house

was at its worst.

"Is she gone?" I asked.

"Yes," Randy told me. He said it quietly. It is masterful the way his eyes look at you—as if he wished to draw the pain drop by drop from your heart. I smiled and told him it didn't matter.

But Sadie came down the stairs. One only has to know how hot it is in this house, with the sound of trapped hornets in the walls to know what I mean. And then there isn't a breath of air. Last night we sat about in our underwear, sweating. My mother wore her bra and shorts, and made Kool-aid. Sadie sat in her nightgown by the window. Harry lay sprawled on the floor. Randy has worn nothing but his bathing-suit these days. I am still in my tight red pants with the slick of grease on the knees. And bare my flat bony chest, hairless except for the teats, to the world.

We sat about the room, each of us lay there in the oddest positions in order to escape the heat, the cry of hornets in the walls, the tick of the fridge and, overall, the smell of oil-cloth.

But the house was filled with agitation. They knew I was on edge because Trenda had left again, and though I tried to be happy it didn't work. No-one looked at me. And then Sadie resumed our war.

"When I was young I had a husband I couldn't stand," Sadie said. "So I used to go for walks at night. All night, in the summer."

No-one answered her.

"Randy, don't you think it's awful the way young people carry on?"

Randy said nothing.

"Well I think it's awful the way young people carry on."

Harry agreed with her. It was very true to him. But I know a particular truth: Sadie kicked him in the testicles when he was a child—so what was he agreeing to?

She talked about the black summer nights at the water's edge, and sang an old song about it. Though she didn't look at me, and our eyes never met, for me there was too much shame in what she was saying.

Norman goes to look for work in the woods. He is gone before daylight, and sometimes he stays until dark. He has no-one, for his wife has left him.

But he will not go to the welfare office.

Nor has he gotten into trouble yet like Jerry.

Trouble that you've never heard.

CHAPTER 3

Harry is on a disability pension. Sometimes he drives Arnold out of the house. Arnold has just come home and wants to make the best of it.

"He has a poor attitude," Arnold thinks.

Harry has taken to saying grace every night, with his fingers held like a church steeple.

"He is quite impressionable," Arnold says one afternoon.

Mabel wants to keep peace now that Arnold has returned. That is her business. And he tries to control his anger.

"Arnold, don't start acting up!"

Don't start acting up.

Arnold knows what is meant by that, and no-one else in the house, not even Randy, knows. The hardest person to get along with is one's self.

Don't start acting up.

He has acted up once. He takes a knife out of the kitchen drawer and slashes his belly. That was five years ago. He is sent away for fourteen days to a hospital, in the northern part of the province. There is desolate tundra and moss on the shore rocks. The earth stops and the sea begins cold and grey, with swells that make your guts freeze, and the cry of gulls. The ribs of a beached ship, its timbers black with ice, lie off shore.

The doors lock behind him. In his room there is a jug of cold water, and a white bed. Every third day he is given linen and asked to change the sheets. They eat three times a day. If you aren't hungry at breakfast no other meal makes up for it. When he goes for walks he walks to the statue of a protestant minister, with two fingers from his right hand broken off.

He learns one must accept things, and learn to get along with oneself. If one is feeling badly he must help the person who has made him feel that way.

Sadie and Harry are sitting on the porch. A dull raincloud has dropped low, but no rain has fallen. The weeds smell sticky, the washtub with the 22 holes through it seems to be visible from any direction.

Harry begins to dye Sadie's hair. He has a tube of black dye, and a plastic wash dish.

"Why doesn't he go away—and take her with him," Arnold thinks.

Harry tells Sadie jokes while he works. He tells the joke, and Sadie bursts out laughing, no matter if the joke is funny or not.

Arnold is sent upstairs to get a mirror and a towel for them. He stays upstairs for as long as possible, gritting his teeth, for the jokes are the worst to bear. He sits on the bed, and looks out the window, across the brown river, and beyond to the naked hills. What a scratch of earth this is. Yet, somedays, it is wise not to want anything. Just this black road.

He hears the jokes Harry tells. All in all they are fairly monotonous jokes. It is going to be a long afternoon with silly jokes crawling into his heart.

Going back downstairs Sadie asks him to work upon her head himself. It is not all unpleasant once he gets at it. The jokes have petered out with a grain of stillness, the fields are dry and the river melts into the low sandbar. The back of Sadie's head looks like a little spittoon. The low raincloud gives rise to the peculiar smell of weeds and rocks associated with his road.

He works upon the head until he is actually doing

something constructive. He is doing everything that ten minutes before he'd thought was disgusting. He even begins tapping his feet. Dyed hair has, he thinks, the smell of varsol. Her skull is very smooth under the thin hair. It is baring itself for the grave. His thumbs are stained and she is chatting away to him, not noticing that Norman is standing on the steps.

When he sees Norman, who looks away, his lips twitching, he becomes too embarrassed to speak. Norman doesn't seem to know what to do. Suddenly he just turns and goes away.

Arnold is watching giraffes on television.

Harry comes in and says:

"I'm watching *Dallas.*"

They glare at each other. It is awful. Their eyes are filled with hatred.

But Harry has his way. Then Sadie comes downstairs. She hauls Randy's ears.

"There you go you little bastard," she yells.

It is as if a full moon has come and gone. Mabel's stomach is hurting again. She complains. She suffers in her big chair. She suffers because of the fighting. She asks Sadie to be quiet, and to leave Randy alone. Randy screams and holds his left ear.

"Randy," Sadie says. "Randy spies on everyone in this goddamn house."

With her hair dyed black she looks crazy. Her ears are still black, and a red bow sits on top of her head.

"I just want to watch my *Dallas,*" Mabel says. You can tell she is suffering. A commercial comes on for Highliner fish. It shows a large portion of fishsticks dancing around a tablecloth, as if they were all down at the recreation centre.

"Randy spies on me—knows my things."

She slaps him across the face. Randy runs upstairs. Mabel finally curls up in her big chair, her face hidden.

Arnold threatens to kick the TV apart.

Then he goes outside. He walks over the heads of the sunflowers. He walks through the wet stinkweed, and across the road. The smell of cowdung is a dangerous smell. He walks along the waggon rut to the water and wades into it. He walks over his head and comes up bobbing like a black fish. The current carries him down to a rock and there he sits. He looks back at the house.

One day follows another. No-one was sure what it was.

Billy the priest caught Harry at something.

"You!" he said. His face was the meanest Arnold had ever seen it.

"Father," Harry said.

"Don't father me," Billy the priest said. He raised his hands in anger and Harry stumbled backwards, gave a defiant squeak and ran into the house. There he sat in the kitchen, hiding, staring out the window.

"Imagine—and he a priest," he said.

To everyone who came in.

"Imagine—a priest—just you imagine."

Mabel comforted him by making him seven pancakes.

Everyone tried to imagine.

But the worst crisis for Arnold, was his girl.

He lay upon the bed thinking of her, while he smoked one cigarette after another. His teeth were black with cigarette stains, as if he enjoyed them looking that way. When a tooth ached, he bit down enjoying the pain.

Juliet came here today to see how Randy was.

How are you making out? she asked him.

He looked at her a second and nodded, as if he were answering yes to a question.

No, I mean how is everything, do you want to tell me?

He nodded again, holding on to his plastic soldier. I felt bad for the grease marks on his neck and stomach. She turned to me when she saw I was nervous.

There is a noise that bottles up our house and makes it sing. It's as prevalent here as rotted oilcloth. I was bothered, but not by her. I have heard that Jerry is wanting to put a beating on me, as soon as he can find me. There are many long filthy afternoons.

I wish someone would let me know what to do. You

don't go to the police. That's like cheating at cards. It isn't easy to protect yourself in this day and age. I can assure you if you've never tried it. Or hold your girlfriend's interest. Especially when you say to her:

"Go on if you want to—go out without me and enjoy yourself." And out she goes. What do you do on these occasions? There's no way out of it.

Juliet's taken an interest in our whole family.

She told Trenda she might be able to go to the west of the province and get a hairdressing course.

She told Sadie she could deliver a meal to her every evening.

She told Mabel what to cook.

She looks at me, and I stare back at her.

But if I show anger I'm in the wrong. If she tells Trenda to go away from me, and I show concern, I'm wrong. As far as the women here are concerned I'm often wrong. If I show argument over the fact she thinks so little of us that she tells my mother what to cook—and just for fun I ask her what *she* cooks, then I'm wrong again. So whenever I look at her she has the upper hand, and I look away. I look away before I start to curse, for Mabel doesn't want trouble. And then I sleep. I'm good at sleeping. I just have to close my eyes.

The whole road knows Jerry.

Jerry wears black pants.

His hair falls before his eyes, as if leading him along.

He walks with a hard stride, side to side, as if he's looking for someone to kick.

But Juliet is no-one to talk to about it.

Before she left she told Randy that there would be a cub pack started here. That the name of the cub-master would be a man named Craig. And that he should see to it that he joined, for he'd find lots of things to do.

Randy nodded once more.

I blinked looking up at her.

What is that noise? she asked.

How do you answer? Doesn't she even know?

What noise—?

There's a noise here. She smiled, rather nicely.
Hornets, I answered. I smiled also.

The priest has asked me to go golfing with him. We are
alone on the sixth fairway. He has asked me here for a
reason but I can't tell what it is.

I carry his bags over my shoulder, and feel like drop-
ping them. It's no good to pretend other people don't
look at my hat, with the feather sticking up, and my pants
that stick to me. Yet when I go back into my underworld
these things don't bother me. I can go to the Arcade, and
be there all day long, playing Outriders, with no-one to
bother me. There are certain youngsters there that look
up to me for my ability. And I can easily compare my
game to his—that is Outriders to golf—and see there is
no comparison.

Why does the priest have such an interest in us?

Who knows.

We sit on a bench in the shade, and let a group of men
go on ahead.

"Are you sure Father," one of the men says.

"No—go ahead—we've all day—go on, we're in no
hurry."

"Why don't you join us—"

(This makes me suspicious.)

"No—we'll wait."

So we wait. And I want to get home.

"Isn't it peaceful here," he says.

I nod, and smile. But it does no good. The sky is so blue
it's lonely. It makes me anxious. It's so clean it makes me
yearn to smell a sewer in the water, a sponge of dirt. The
birds, on little sticklike legs, hop closer to us.

A shadow glides over the earth. It makes me think of
the story the social worker read me when I was a child,
waiting to go to family court, of Aladdin flying over
Baghdad with his tragic pints of gold. "How would you
like to have all that money?" she'd asked me. This is what
I think of.

Juliet is our social worker.

Billy is our priest.

Even they don't see eye to eye on how we're supposed to live.

Juliet constantly talks to Mabel.

As if this talking might settle everything.

Anyway the women at home have turned against me.

One at a time.

The priest asks me strange questions. He is leading up to something.

"What do you think of the prison?"

"All right—if someone can get a job at it."

"Well," the priest says, "you know why they put the prison on our road do you?"

"Sure, to give us some jobs."

"No, they put the prison here because no-one else in the entire country wanted it—and made sure they didn't get it."

I don't know what to think about it. As always I try to answer them to please them, so the questions will stop coming, but there are more questions than answers today.

The priest has brought ginger ale in his golf bag and treats me. He treats me to a chicken sandwich that is the best I've ever tasted.

"They make them here—at the golf club," he tells me. It is the most delicious sandwich in the world to me. If I didn't live 40 miles away, I would walk here every day in order to get one.

As always, whatever the priest asks I answer, and smile. I look at the ground, which is black, rich and torn by cleats.

There are only two things I can think of.

That he has heard Harry and I have had a fight—and he has heard that I tried to drown myself when I walked into the river. This isn't true, but it didn't stop the RCMP from questioning me about it. It is hard to look people in the eye and tell them you didn't attempt to kill yourself. It poses a lot of difficulty, especially when their eyes are coldly set upon you, coldly size you up for some sort of deficiency. This is how the RCMP questioned me, when they took me to the office.

"Well," they told me, "it's good to have people worried about you isn't it. They reported it because they didn't want anything to happen to you."

"What would happen?"

"Perhaps things are getting to be difficult," the officer said.

"I have no difficulty," I said.

This went on for a little bit with them. I knew when I left the headquarters, and walked away, they still watched me, as if I were going to jump in front of a truck or something. But nothing like that has crossed my mind in days.

The other thing the priest might ask me about is if Trenda sunbathed with her top off, showing her little white teats to the world—though I asked her not to.

The priest does ask me something very quickly, while I'm still thinking of Trenda and how she lay with her teats in the air, and still biting my chicken sandwich, and trying to chew it without making a noise.

"Is Jerry bothering you?" he asks.

My mouth goes dry and I look across the fairway. Far away the men who left us are like toys, striding under the fierce sun.

The blue sky.

A blueness like horror.

Father Billy has a bloated face and big conical ears. He sits beside my skinny body holding a 3-wood in his hand.

"Not at all," I say.

"If he does go to the police and get a court order against him. You have to protect yourself you know."

"Yes," I say. But what is a court order?

I shrugged. I didn't know why he asked the question. I thought he was going to ask something else. The only thing I know about Jerry is that Jerry is his own worst enemy.

But I never allow myself to think of it.

And I'm still glad I don't think about the Norwegian

who was murdered, one way or the other.

The priest looks at me strangely, and looks away. The wax paper my sandwich came in blows away in a sudden hot gust, and dust blows up happily under our feet.

"Well maybe I can hit a half decent drive," he says.

I smile and pick his bags up.

But my heart isn't in the game.

CHAPTER 4

Father Billy told him his family had no determination left to make its mark on the world. It slept. The days passed, one, two, three, as if they were nothing. Sadie slept in the best room in the house, all alone, her hair dyed, with a ribbon in it. Harry slept in the kitchen (there was a cot by the stove and he slept there almost always). Mabel slept. Or when her stomach hurt she walked the floor cursing. The TV, lone occupant of the living-room, remained burning. The light in the upstairs hallway burned yellow. The taps in the bathroom and the pipe behind the toilet dripped.

When they woke, when they stirred, the old lady would start to sing:

"I'm just Sadie
The cleaning-lady
I'm just Sadie
The cleaning-lady—"

It wouldn't be long before a confrontation occurred. Arnold would shout:

"Shut up crazy arse—I'm trying to sleep."

There'd be silence for a moment or two, and then:

"I'm still Sadie—
Still a cleaning-lady—
Sadie's all I am."

"She's singing the cleaning-lady song again," Randy

would whisper.

"You be quiet too!"

Often they would all slumber off again. For another day. Time passed with or without them. Now and then there was a stir on the road, some big deal was going on, and they would have the misfortune of sleeping through it.

Somedays the whole household was in a foul mood. One of those moods when not even the priest came forward to talk to them, and no social worker turned the door-handle. And they waited for someone to make a move, a mistake, or to do something out of the ordinary, so the rest could pounce on them and make their life less attractive.

The afternoon Randy came home with his cub cap, and a book called *Cub Scouting in America,* how they looked at him. First with a sly look.

"You think you're some big with that on," Sadie said.

"Big shot," Harry said.

"I am not a big shot."

"Big shot," they said in unison.

"Let me see your cap," Harry said.

"No—you're just making fun of me—all of you."

Randy held on to his head.

They glared at him. How saucy he was.

"You get to bed," Mabel screeched.

Randy then backed away, stared at everyone and put up his arms as if to defend himself.

How a child runs so awkwardly, it's enough to make you snicker.

Randy started to run away.

"Get him," Harry said.

"Don't trip him on the stairs," Mabel warned.

The cap flew off. Arnold snatched it up and paraded about with it on. Randy tried to grab it, but Harry and Seaweed threw it back and forth over his head.

Later, everyone stayed out of each other's way. Arnold went upstairs. Randy slept, with his cub scouting book hidden under a pillow so black you were afraid to breathe into it.

Perhaps he should have protected him from their bad mood. But bad moods were inevitable, like storms. But out of a storm you could make something beautiful.

Arnold twisted and was nervous for days after. He was sick to his stomach and took to his bed. Because his mother was sick they fought for the bathroom. There was no happiness in the last bit of summer for him. The pains in his head increased.

There seemed to be no meals made in the summer months. The old lady, Sadie, was being fed by the community. She had a hot meal each day. She sat in her bedroom, with a tray, and a napkin tucked under her chin. She made sure she left the door open so she could talk to those who walked by her. Arnold, it was true, was a little envious when he saw her.

Mabel had fed them all for years. But now she couldn't anymore. The supper went uncooked, and even Harry was on his own. But Sadie often said:

"Mabel never did a thing for me."

She told this to Juliet, who brought the hot meal.

She told this to Harry, who sat dejected in the corner of the bedroom, breathing in hard little puffs, and watching her eat spaghetti.

"She doesn't feed me either," Harry would say, looking at his shoes.

Or

"When am I gonna get fed?"

Or

"At least you got a meal Sadie—at least you got a meal."

There was always food. Seaweed ate it only when he didn't fill up on pop and chips at Johnson's Arcade. Harry would open the fridge and look at it, turn up his nose and close the fridge again. He wouldn't have enough gumption to take it out and cook it. He'd grab a bag of jelly beans instead, and sit in the living-room hiding them from Randy. He wasn't the cleanest man in the world either, but he was the first to complain about Randy's feet, especially when they were in sneakers all

37

day.

This would drive Mabel to climb the stairs and get a pot of water to bathe Randy's feet. Randy would yell at his mother, his mother would curse at him. Harry would sit in the big chair.

Harry would sit in the big chair until Juliet came with the food for his mother, and then he'd open the door. He'd smile and say,

"Yes—please come in."

Or

"September is coming—is that a September sweater— do you have a September sweater?"

Sadie would be upstairs waiting, with her napkin.

Harry would run all over the house for the woman. So when she said:

"Is there a knife here?"

Harry would say:

"Is there a knife here—why I guess there's a knife here—"

And he would run and fetch one.

When she said:

"How's your mom?"

he would look at her.

"Mommy's ill," he would say. Then he'd try to cry, as if this was expected of him. Seaweed noticed he was an emotional fellow, who could cry whenever he wanted.

"The poor soul," Juliet would say.

Sadie would wait with her napkin, tapping her feet on the floor.

Juliet had long hair, fluffy as a cat's tail, with the odour of soap. She had poor eyes and wore thick-rimmed glasses.

Arnold decided that he didn't like her. She liked Sadie too much, and that was a mark against her.

He learned something else. From the road.

She had her own problems as if she were human. However what did that matter?

Someone was always running your life. It may as well be her as someone else. And though he heard her speak out, and say things that weren't true, he said nothing. For what is there to say?

"Trenda has come back to you," Mabel tells me, "you should be happy—and stop questioning where she's been."

"Have you ever showed your teats to the world," I say. I'm in a bad mood. My hair hasn't been washed in a month, and I've been too lazy to swim. I go about the house in a bad mood. Ready to fight.

"Don't talk filth in this house," Mabel says.

It is a rainy night, and the rain floods the ditches down below our house.

Everyone thinks I tried to drown myself because of Trenda. That's a possibility. I can say nothing to her. She wears a bright little costume, shorts that show most of her behind, but I say nothing, a scarf that hangs from her throat, but I don't mind, a bracelet that I will tell you I think is a stolen bit of equipment—and I know where she got it, but my lips are sealed.

She is teaching Randy to dance. And she tries to coax me onto the floor also. She holds his hands, and leads him about the living-room, and encourages him to twist his body. I'm swept by physical pain when I think of everything. I refuse to budge.

A skinny man, not more than 5′2″ does not deserve a healthy woman anyway.

A man without hair is an oddball on this road.

Even Harry has hair.

And Sadie has a little moustache.

A man without hair on his chest or belly is a lonely thing, his own worst enemy.

A hairless man's shame starts below his chin on this road.

He has no-one to blame but himself.

There is a repulsive stickiness with the rain. It enters our house and makes it damp. When Trenda dances she moves her buttocks in a way that makes men weak.

I sit on the stairs.

I go nowhere without my own thoughts.

I've lost too much time thinking of things.

For the police are watching me—

They want to talk to me about something—and I will tell you what.

All last winter and into spring, the vault in the church-yard was being robbed. The coffins opened and jewellery and even clothing taken.

Jerry has eyes that look right inside you. When he gets angry there is nothing in them, as if you are trying to find a soul in them and find none because he is sucking your soul out of you. And then he smiles. He was born here a short nineteen years ago, and has lived here all along.

I don't think he has gone out to Calgary, as so many of us have, or gone anywhere else.

This road is his home. He knows every family. He knows every tree. The only one he might fear is Norman —but he knows too, he would kill Norman in a second if no-one would be wise to it. And he has lived beside us. He has lived in back of us. He has lived wherever I have.

It was he who began to call me Seaweed when he came to town one day. I try to be pleasant to him.

For there was once a sailor who disappeared in town. A Norwegian sailor. Jerry lived in the hotel at that time. Now the investigation has gone on for three years. The family in Norway has sent letters to the paper, offering a reward. There is only silence.

There is only silence from this dark road, that splits two counties in the north of the province.

Jerry looks at me.

Or beyond me to his own torment.

However, I keep my mouth shut about that, and I keep it shut about the vault being robbed.

Jerry, however, has been watching me a long time.

His boots are coarse and steel-toed.

And I've seen him kick a wounded deer to death.

My head's as little as a doe's—so I would do good to carry a knife again.

Someone must have buried the Norwegian on the

beach, knowing the waves and ice would wash over him, and take his body out to sea.

I hear the rain hitting the tin bucket in Sadie's room, and washing against the oil barrel with its soup can over the cylinder. I think of nights alone and peaceful.

The police wish to question me about the vault. Well let them.

I think Trenda is a stupid girl, dancing so carefree with the bracelet upon her arm.

No smell of death invades our house tonight. In fact the little bells on the bracelet jingle a merry lively song.

CHAPTER 5

His mother loves one song. She sings it to give herself peace, and plays it on the record player. Her face lights up with happiness when she hears it:

"The Wayward Wind."

By Gogi Grant.

No-one else likes it. Everyone else hates it. They sit around the living-room, hating to look at one another when his mother is at her happiest.

Mabel can't sing, she can't carry a tune, as everyone knows. But she prolongs their agony by singing along with it, and makes a nuisance of herself by tapping her pudgy fingers to the tune.

But whose house is it?

It doesn't seem like their house now. Neither Mabel nor he is in charge. It is the same colour as it has been over the last ten years. It is dirty red. It has a splash of green here and there, but it is red for the most part. It is as if they wished to show the house a good time by painting it that colour, but even they can't fool it. Dusty crab grass surrounds it. And under the house lie things, for years on end. An old scythe lay there until Randy cut his foot open on it.

"What was it doing there?"

No-one knew.

But for some reason it was good to joke about stitching toes.

The men sat in the living-room, yelling at television programs they didn't like. No-one talked to their television more than he or Harry. Day or night they had something to say to their television.

"Get away," Harry would laugh.

"Go on—go on," he would yell.

"What do you mean by that?"

They never seemed to know what was making them so angry with television. But something did. Something deep in what the television was saying angered them and made them abusive.

When Juliet heard this yelling and cursing one afternoon, she was overwhelmed.

"Be overwhelmed," Arnold said, "be overwhelmed all you goddamn want."

"Yes," Harry said, taking his side for once, "be overwhelmed—go and overwhelm yourself—shithead."

They turned back to the TV in unison, and went right on yelling and cursing.

Juliet went upstairs with the meal.

Didn't she know that the TV lied.

Lied about them.

Lied about the province.

Lied about Arnold himself.

Or did she think that the TV told the truth—

He was shaking. He was angry.

He went upstairs.

"What are you doing in my house?" he yelled.

Sadie had her white napkin tucked all the way around her, as if she was in town at the barber's.

"I'm hired by the province," Juliet said calmly, "if you want to take it up with someone—take it up with the Provincial Government—"

"Provincial Government," Arnold said, "whose Provincial Government?"

He bit his lip blue, he was so angry. The woman smiled calmly at him. He'd seen that smile before. He'd seen it everywhere, he'd seen it in family court also. He'd seen it anywhere there were people who lived the way she did.

"Provincial Government," he said, "Provincial Government—go away from here before I get mad, leave us alone—or you'll be sorry."

Juliet said nothing.

That was the end of the argument. He slammed the door.

"Do you want the door opened Sadie?"

"Yes please—I like to eat my dinner with the door opened."

He was embarrassed at flying off the handle, and didn't look at her when she left the house. Besides, the whole household suddenly took her side:

"Don't start trouble—watch yourself," Mabel said.

"Why should I watch myself," he said, cursing and staring at his feet. But ever since he'd slashed himself for seventeen stitches he'd tried to take other people's advice. He'd done nothing right.

Courage is essential—Norman said.

Norman had courage.

No-one would bother Norman.

It was always that way.

The first to whimper was Harry.

He whimpered.

And Mabel whimpered.

Christ, what a bunch. They were all like sheep— although he hardly knew what a sheep looked like, he'd always heard what sheep were like.

"Arnold," said his mother, "why don't you say you're sorry."

"Yes," Harry said, "be sorry once in awhile, why don't you."

What cowards we all are he thought.

"I don't want trouble," Mabel said. "She's legal."

There was nothing more to be said.

43

My mother's birthday makes me ill. She wants everyone to wear a party hat, as if we were really friendly with one another. But none of us are in a particularly good mood, so why hats? Why not bats? Sadie's hat slowly falls down below her eyes, and Harry's sits upon his head like a cone.

She wants, my mother, everyone to tell her a story, about last year—that is, what they thought of last year.

Is the social worker right, she asks.

Sadie says she is.

Harry says the social people have made important changes.

This is Canada, Sadie says.

Important changes, Harry says.

Randy says he wants cake and ice cream.

I say nothing. It is almost autumn and I smell how my mother has suffered. I smell it in her eyes. I smell it in her coat that will be taken out and worn to bingo and church. The bitter talk of the social worker and the priest.

Mabel says she is tricked by people.

That's just doctors darling, Sadie says.

Yes, doctors trick me, she replies.

More than anything else my mother has fought and sometimes whined to get money for us from the welfare office. Tonight she wears a brown paper hat with a picture of a clown, and cuts deep into the cake.

This is Canada, Harry says.

I'll never go to the hospital again, Mabel says, I'll get better myself—it's only my diet.

If you go to the hospital again, you'll die.

Do you know I have adhesions—and they're strangling my bowels.

But none of us know anything about it.

I won't come out of another operation.

She shows us the scars, the scars of one year. I can still smell the heat off them.

I want cake and ice cream, Randy says.

Do you love me, Mabel says.

Of course we love you dear—

Of course darling we love you.

I don't know if I have a friend in the world—we never see eye to eye, or do anything together.

Of course we do, Sadie says, we do lots together.

I promise, Harry says, from now on it will be different.

You know we are the only ones on this road who suffer so much.

That's the government's fault, I say, for some reason.

CHAPTER 6

Autumn was here. He could smell it in the smoke at night. He could smell it in Randy's hair. He could hear it in Randy's teeth as he bit into a cold apple. He smelled it in the birdnests that he cleaned from the chimney.

Night came earlier. The water lay still. It lay still here, and it lay still on the main river. It lay still in the bay. The great ships came and went, listing with their cargo, but the mill was closing. As if to let everyone know it was closing it gave out gasps of sulphur that could be tasted in any direction.

Grass lay silent.

Women looked lonely walking from church.

The potholes and the black road, the chopped over hills beyond, remained much the same.

Trenda gave him a deadly look one evening, which only a man knows; it was the look that said he had lost her, and not anything mattered beyond that.

She was eighteen now, and very beautiful, he thought.

"I'm going away," she said.

He didn't even ask her why. He stared at her.

He began talking.

"You know," he said, "I thought we'd have a place of our own someday—you know, better than this, and have things, in the back of this place for instance—like we'd have trees and stuff, and a swing, to swing our kid, and then we'd have a pool—a little pool like for fish—and bees come and go—"

Trenda stared at him as she smoked a cigarette. Then she inspected her boots to see if there was any dust or mud on them. And then she yawned.

He put his head down. Then he grabbed the feather out of his hat and broke it to pieces.

"Don't mess with me—hey you—hey you," he yelled. He busted the feather apart like he'd never busted it apart previously. It might as well not have been his good luck feather at all for how he treated it.

"I'm just a different person—a different,—a different woman."

Trenda said. She lighted a cigarette, and held it in her pink fingers. She held it, and dragged upon it, and let the smoke curl softly out of her beautiful lips.

He bit his tongue when he looked at her.

And what had he been watching;

"*Hill Street Blues.*"

It was all a mess. His breath was sharp, and each breath pained him. He didn't want to hear anything more—yet he was fascinated by her.

"Well then," he stammered, "you'll be sorry."

But she looked at him as if she wasn't sorry at all.

Then two big tears rolled from his eyes, and he licked them away when they hit the corner of his mouth.

The commercial where the Highliner fish-sticks are square-dancing consoled him for a moment. He sniffed and shook like a faulty piece of machinery as he watched it.

"I've made up my mind," Trenda said. "There are other ways to live."

He said nothing, but he always knew there was a cruel streak in her and now it was coming out. She said:

"You don't know how many people love me—"

Arnold smiled at this. He continued to smile, biting on his teeth until he loosened one. He bit down until all his gums bled red, and blood smeared his lips. He rubbed his fingers through his hair, smiling at her.

His shoulders flinched. Trenda said:

"Maybe I'll move out west—maybe I'll take a hairdressing course—maybe I'll see you around too."

There was a little light left from the September evening. It finished itself on the window-sill, and against the big chair. It smelled of the cold tractors that sat in the fields without running. Of the rocks that turned cold in the mud. It languished on his good-luck feather that lay upon the floor like a broken wing.

"Arnold," she said, "your whole mouth is bloody—why look, you broke a tooth—get to the bathroom."

She butted one cigarette, and lit another.

"There," she said, "another one—another tooth, there it goes."

And truly he bit at his teeth until two or three rotted ones broke—and fell to the floor, one rolling under his foot.

CHAPTER 7

The nights, the change of weather, all was colder now. The earth settled into itself, and the house creaked at night.

Some people said she was running around on him.

And others said nothing.

Norman said he shouldn't think of her.

But it bothered him. It came into his head and wouldn't leave him alone. So he had a drink or two.

"Listen," Cy Ramsey told him, "do you still love her—"

"Of course not."

The man laughed and told him a story about Trenda. Her own father, he said, took pictures of Trenda when she was fourteen and sold them.

"She was naked—those pictures are still around."

The man couldn't help laughing when he saw that this bothered the boy.

"People should stop bothering me," Arnold said. But the man thought nothing about this.

Cy Ramsey owned a pit from where he sold gravel. And a few acres of Maritime spruce. Cy winked and drank his beer. "She isn't the girl for you—even her old man sold pictures of her—and now Jerry is screwing her."

"Leave me alone," Arnold said.

The man only laughed and bought Arnold a beer, and when Arnold got drunk, he said things he shouldn't have. He said that Jerry killed the Norwegian. He didn't remember saying this. But such was his thinking. Cy coughed into his beer and said nothing.

"She was in a little dress," Cy kept saying. He smelled of rancid chewing-tobacco. But this was no problem. "A cute little dress, without anything on underneath—it's a good picture—you want to see it? A cute little butt on her then."

Arnold thought he was going to be sick. Then he said he could get some people with a knife very easily. He didn't remember saying this either, but there was a pain in his head.

Cy kept buying him beer, and when he went home the only thing he could think of was the little dress. And how people treated her. Then he sat on the stairs for a while. Then he hit Randy over the neck with a judo chop, and sent him flying, and he had no reason to do this.

He went out to town to see her. All his resolution not to see her again failed. He had known it would fail. His mother grabbed at his arm crying.

Mabel had cried over herself.

She had cried over losing her money.

She had cried over *Another World*.

She had cried when Sadie called her a slut.

But she had not cried over her children.

No, she hadn't shed a tear over her children. And Seaweed knew this. Her eyes this time though were

48

moist, and the yellow light of the porch shone on them.

"Arnold," she cried.

Yet why didn't he like it, now that she was crying? Why was there not an ounce of peace in his heart as she clutched onto him?

"Don't go," Mabel said, "you'll get into trouble!"

"Go away," he said.

"Arnold," she pleaded, "don't start trouble!"

"Go away."

Had she not admired men who made trouble he thought. And didn't the world itself admire men who made trouble? And didn't women think it advisable to start trouble?

These thoughts came to mind, and he couldn't unravel them for they would bite him. He knew one thing, and he told his mother this:

"You should get out to the hospital again," he said, "before your insides are too damaged."

He walked down to the road, and began to walk along it. He walked along it quickly. The dark surrounded him, as silent as any road in Canada—as dark as any also. His house was separated from other houses by woods. Each house was separated by spruce woods, each wood was hot enough to blister the trees and burst seed in summer and cold enough to close hot bloody wounds in winter. He never asked himself why his ancestors came here, to this inch or so of soil.

Each wood separated a house.

And each house was admired by him more than his own.

And the dark surrounded him. He walked, yet it seemed he was going nowhere in a hurry.

"I'm going to town," he thought, "to see if she has come to her senses!"

A little farther on he thought:

"What am I smelling—a swamp—a cesspool?"

A little farther on he saw a light before his eyes, but it was only the glow of his own cigarette.

He stopped a moment. Perhaps someone was following behind? He tried not to breathe, yet he found it impossible. One must breathe—especially when one is walking.

"What stupidity."

He moved slowly off, into the September night.

After a certain time came more houses. And a little farther on, the smell that was so encouraging in this dark land, the smell of sulphur, which everyone knew.

A meteor fell through the sky, and burnt out, Arnold thought, at his feet. In the last week, he'd taken to looking for signs from heaven for things also. He pondered this as he walked with his hands deep in his pockets. He'd taken off his red pants not too long ago, and had thrown them into the corner of his bedroom, and had put on a pair of pea-green ones—which were too large for him. His legs were lost in them. They seemed to drag behind him and slow him down.

The towers of the mill came into view.

And its clay windows.

And the streets of the town with its dark shadows.

When he found her that evening (she was sitting in a tavern with a group of young women) no words came from his mouth. He tried to look stern—but smiled.

Only people from his province couldn't speak to defend themselves. Hadn't others told his mother what to do? Hadn't Trenda told him what to do? In fact didn't she tell him she liked green pants—pea-green, with brass buttons up the front, instead of a zipper? Hadn't she told him to hate certain people? Of course he would hate people for her—he would hate anyone for her.

Yet, she wanted him to hate Norman.

But he didn't hate Norman. Did he even believe her anymore—that it was Norman who robbed his mother?

Yes he decided with great resolution as he sat down near the rear door that he would hate Norman if she wanted. He looked over at them all smiling and winking.

This was the first tavern. They stood and ran from him. He followed them through the midly lighted streets. Everything was strange. Another tavern; he followed them inside, only to find they had gone out the back way, and across a lot. Each one of the girls—there were four—walked with her hair bouncing up and down, each one looked behind her, just an instant, and each one whispered into Trenda's ear.

He gathered all his courage:

"Trenda," he said smiling, "it's me—Arnold."

He called after them:

"Come back for a drink of beer."

And took money out of his pocket. Some dirty white coins fell through his fingers.

One of the girls came back.

"You've made her cry."

"Who has?"

"You have—you have, with your mean tongue."

"Let me talk to her—I have a thing or two to say."

Her white lips quivered, at the very ends of her mouth. Seaweed's lips quivered.

"She has friends now—good friends," the girl said, "you won't treat her that way again." She spoke loud enough so everyone could hear, and as if she wanted them to. Suddenly a smell of salt blew from the water. Salt and dead fish, and the human dump. How beautiful it was, to smell all things in the earth this way.

He looked away.

"I know all about it," Arnold said, suddenly, "I'm Arnold—you don't mess with me." He threw his money into the dirt.

The girl looked behind her. Then she turned and walked quickly away. He walked behind her, almost on her heels, yelling, "I'm the one who'll do the talking," and waving his arms.

"We're here," Trenda yelled. "Run."

And suddenly the girl screamed and began to run.

"Hurry Janet we're here—over here."

And Janet screamed.

Trenda screamed from behind a fish barrel.

Arnold ran behind her, for a foot or two.

What were they screaming about; it was absurd. No-one should scream.

"I'm Seaweed," he yelled. "Just as always."

He stayed at home for a week after. Nothing was going to get him outside again. The nights turned calm and cool, the stars were bright.

Mabel was feeling better, and so she cooked a stew and everyone ate and enjoyed themselves. Randy wore his cub cap around the house and no-one said anything. Mabel showed Arnold letters his father received from relatives in Maine ten years ago, and Arnold read them. Arnold read these letters, and thought that maybe he would go to Rumford Falls, and see his relatives 250 miles south. But then he forgot about it. He thought of Trenda.

She had run away from him.

The girls had run. They had stamped their feet.

And someone said, "She's behind a fish barrel crying her sweet eyes out."

And he felt ashamed.

Tears came to his eyes, but they were colder than the first tears he had cried.

Sadie sang:

"She's someone else's lover—

Though he thinks she's being true—"

Mabel pleaded with her to stop.

Sadie stopped. But it didn't matter. He sat in the big chair. Harry wanted to sit in it. Arnold stared at him with such a look on his face, Harry said:

"I think you're mean—Sadie said I could."

"Could what?" Arnold asked.

"Sit in the good chair—Sadie said. She said I could have it all day."

Arnold blinked and looked away.

Mabel was content to have Harry here—in a room that whispered with the autumn wind, in a house where they pinned souvenirs on the wall, on a road that never ended.

And the souvenirs weren't much good for anything. What did they ever tell you? It made you tired to look at them. Little plates and a cup sat on a shelf. They'd sat there so long they'd yellowed. A picture of the Queen.

"But what does the Queen care," was a standard line Sadie used, and everyone knew what she meant without even knowing anything about the Queen, England, the Commonwealth of Nations—without knowing even where this little province began and ended.

"But what does the Queen care," was Sadie's line—and everyone respected her for it.

A flashy picture of Bruce sat upon the TV. He was smiling. And he'd signed his name: "Love ya Mabel"—exactly what Mabel had asked him to sign when he came to the spring auto show.

Arnold thought about Bruce now and again. For instance, what was he doing at just this second? It was hard to contemplate when there was so much trouble in the house, with everyone flying off the handle at one another, it was hard to think how Bruce was doing.

Bruce was a TV personality.

Mabel called him a movie star.

He made girls swoon on TV. There was no other way to say it. And he had all girls in a deep swoon. Mabel too. He'd seen how giddy she was after she'd talked to him. Bruce had tickled her chin with a finger. She was giddy for a week. She sat on the sofa and all her problems may as well not have existed. But then, after she snapped out of it, a depression overcame her.

Her belly was sore.

Her backside was as huge as ever—like a bumblebee's.

Her face was as white and as drawn as codfish.

Trenda told people he was simpleminded.

So people began to call him that when he went to the Arcade.

He worried until the pains in his head became intolerable. He knew this was wrong thinking.

"I don't want to be called Seaweed," he would say, for no reason, at the most obscure hours.

"He doesn't want to be called Seaweed," Randy would

yell.

"What's that?" Sadie would interject.

"Arnold," Randy would say, "I'm goin' out to cubs."

"Who doesn't want to be called what?" Sadie would ask.

As soon as Randy left, Sadie would come forward, from her bedroom, down the dark stairs.

Everything would be quiet.

Everything would be nice.

Hawaii Five-O would be on television.

"Treat a woman bad she'll run away—"

"Shh," Mabel would say.

"Treat a woman bad, like that fellow Norman did, like a doormat—she'll run—Seaweed—that's your problem."

"Shut up."

"Your only problem—is—I bet you beat her up."

"What did you say?"

"You beat her on the head."

"He did no such thing."

"He beat her—treated the poor little thing like a doormat," Sadie said. She was very polite, and tried not to blow smoke in his face.

"I never," Seaweed said. He couldn't look at anyone.

Sadie said:

"I could tell, Seaweed I could always tell." She yawned and settled back to watch TV.

And she began to tap her foot. Tap, tap. She had fleshed out from 50 hot meals, and was beginning to bare her teeth.

He'd go out along the wet fields with his eyes cold. He'd walk down the blacktop road, with its tortuous tire marks, and trucks would have to sound their horns. He'd move just enough, but no more. His clothes would be almost sucked off him.

"Whew," Randy would say, "that was close."

"What was close?"

"You crossed the road right in front of that truck."

"Oh—did I?"

"I yelled, 'Get out of the way Arnold—run and jump.'"

"Did you?"

54

"I yelled 'Holy ol frig Arnold—ya'll be squished.'"

"Did you?"

Randy wore his woollen cub sweater about the yard. He had two badges.

"When I get four badges, I can go into the woods and stay all night."

"For what?"

"For to stay all night."

"Why?"

"Cubs are the types of people to do that."

These were the things Randy was interested in. Arnold was interested in nothing.

Juliet ignored him, though he knew she was watching everything he did.

He didn't believe, as they all did, that things had gotten better since the social workers began to organize existence for them. Nor did he want to believe this. But when she stared at him, he had to look away—as if he were being hit. He would stare out the window, or at the steeple of the Catholic Church, which was called "Our Lady of the Gladdened Heart."

It was a little parish—a stinkingly small one—one road, one Indian reserve, one priest.

The church was tucked away in some trees. Its yard was quiet. It softly waited out the days. It had a quiet gate that opened and closed for coffins. There was a small garden in back of the parish house. It had rows that were ripened and turned over. It sat above a small pool on the river, right at the bend.

"Why are you staring at me?" he asked Juliet one afternoon.

"I?"

"Yes you."

"I'm not staring at you. Someone is paranoid."

"You'd better watch it."

Juliet smiled.

"Ha," Seaweed said. He sat on the couch.

Juliet looked at him.

"You're being obnoxious today Arnold."

She touched the middle of her glasses with a pointed finger.

"I know whose house this is—that's all."

"Is Mabel in?"

"Ha."

"Yes Arnold?"

"Mabel sees you coming—she runs out the back door—"

He kept looking out of the corner of his eye at her, and then glancing away.

"I think you and I can get along so much better."

"Ha."

"Don't start today," Harry pleaded.

Arnold said:

"Ha."

Juliet looked at him calmly. Harry blew his nose for something to do. A nose-blowing session that was filled with piety.

"Seaweed," Harry said, "Seaweed."

"I'm not paranoid," Seaweed said, suspiciously. "I bet no-one even knows what that is."

CHAPTER 8

What am I afraid of?

I am not afraid.

I listen to the radio, which is on now as much as the television. No-one bothers to turn anything off, and the radio can go for days without anyone thinking too much about it. Its little digital clock keeps the time, which seems to be running out around here.

Mabel has come back from the hospital. She went there overnight. If they tell her anything she believes them. She smiles at the doctor. She won't say boo to a doctor, and I get sick of listening to her diet plans. I get sick when

I see how she tells the doctor lies.

"How are you?" the doctor asks.

"Not too bad," she says.

In front of him she is a mealy-mouth. When she dies she will die. If they tell her she is to suffer, she will suffer. That's all there is to it. It's because she knows no better, and I have no right to talk about it.

"Fuck," I said, "tell them your belly hurts!"

"Don't you think they know!"

"Ask the doctor to give you some advice. An injection or something."

"The doctor knows what's what—you're just like your father, you get upset over nothing—"

"You're a big-tool lover aren't you."

So I make her cry. She has put her winter coat back on to spite anyone who hates her. She sits about the house with the radio on day and night, just like the television. Maybe the radio tells us things we should know, but I don't think it tells us anything important. So, when Mabel listens to it, I'm not in the mood to listen to it.

Canada has become a force in the theatre.

There is a new choreographer doing wonderful things in Ottawa.

The government lost 20 million dollars on eggs.

We have bought a new plane for our air-force, and already the plane has cracks in its wings. A billion dollars worth of cracks.

I don't know if this bothers me or not.

So I say to her:

"You won't get many at your funeral—not as many as the old man!"

She looks at me and smiles like a little girl who is afraid.

"No, you won't have a big funeral at all—because you're a tramp—a bingo-loving bitch!"

This is how we talk to each other when no-one is around. When there are no social workers or priests to tell us to be gentle.

Juliet was angry with us, and we haven't seen her in two days now. I don't know how she got angry with us—but

57

we aren't doing something she thinks we should be. Our phone has been disconnected because we ran up a bill. One night last month we called everyone we could think of, the people in Maine and people in Toronto Harry knew, and we didn't pay for it. But what's a phone? Then she had arranged a job interview for me to sweep up again at the theatre, but I rolled over that morning and went back to sleep. There is something that Juliet doesn't know—that people cut each other open just for spite and you can't apply any words to it. The more you apply words, the more there is misunderstanding.

Sometimes I sit on the cot all day, just for peace. I know the moods of my family. It's in the dry barren trees that have afforded us no money. It's in the soil, rancid and spoiled with too many widgits of human equipment.

Sometimes I talk to Randy about this. But I can get nothing out of him.

"Why do you go to cubs?"

"Because I want to."

"You stupid little weasel."

He says nothing.

"Craig doesn't like you—he has it in for you."

"My neck is too skinny—I have to build it up."

Craig told him he had to build his neck muscles, so he is lifting weights after school. He looks determined when he tells me this. His face is set, his fists clenched, yet the others can blow on him and he'd fall down. No-one here taught us how to box. No-one here taught us how to use weights. It's better to carry a knife.

I know all about how people treat one another.

Yesterday I came upon Randy in our room. He had finally trapped a certain number of hornets and with a little shriek was banging them across their luglike bodies with a hammer. The night was grey, and rain came in through the open window and ran from the window-sill to the floor where a few of the dead hornets floated. His neck looked like a stick in the warm wind, and I watched how the hornets tried to crawl away on their abysmal torn legs or fly with crushed wings.

Now and then he picked one up angrily and tore it apart in his hands.

Jerry asks me to go for a drive. We are travelling close to the ground. I smell Trenda in the car.

"The last time I was in the provincial jail," Jerry tells me, "Monroe took my clothes—he said I was a bad apple and wouldn't let me out of my cell, unless I was taking a shower. I had to sit in my cell for four months—I don't want to go back there again."

"So you should have told someone."

He looks at me with eyes that have lost their fear of killing.

"I'm telling *you*—just because of Trenda don't become a rat."

He thinks I'm a rat, and that's the worst thing. There's no protection for you when someone thinks this.

"If you killed the Norwegian—that's nothing to me." I tell him this while he's looking right at me and shrug as I do.

I think of Trenda's fingernails as painted little swords, the earrings she wears as teardrops, the colour of blood.

"I don't talk about you at all," I tell him. I see that he is scared now—frightened of that night that he and the Norwegian spent alone.

"Someone might have a big mouth on them," he tells me.

"About what?"

"About things that happened that are best forgotten."

About the wind perhaps. About the sad nights in the back of cars perhaps. About all the things in a lifetime that are best not thought of. We drive and I stare at the grey little stones at the open mouth of the ditches, the plastic curtains drawn over the blank September windows.

He tells me that there is a window above the shower-stall in the provincial jail.

"Even if I have to go out of that window naked, the next time I'm there I'll go."

59

I think of Jerry running through the black snow, with steam coming off his back. There would be so much energy when he ran that I think of this. All that trouble, just to get away.

"I'm getting a few tattoos of my own," I say.

CHAPTER 9

Randy would let out long sighs, for no reason, at the supper table. Arnold tried to remain calm, but on occasion it was a hard thing to master.

The night he fought with Sadie he realized that she was like an old crow who had grown up fighting owls.

That she fought with a desperation that must have come from fighting husbands.

It started politely enough.

"Where's Mom's record?" he asked politely.

She didn't answer.

"Where's Mabel's record of 'the Wayward Wind'?" he asked.

"Seaweed—never mind," Mabel said. "Don't start trouble."

"She hid it."

"Hid what—what did I hide—what!" Sadie snapped.

"You hid Gogi Grant."

"Ha," Sadie said.

There was silence for a second. Silence that can only be bettered by a hurricane.

"Find it," Sadie said.

"I'll find it."

"Ha."

"Don't forget yourself," Mabel said.

"Ha—Seaweed needs a doctor," Sadie said. "He's peer-a-nod."

"I'll find it," Arnold said, his lips trembling.

She had a nice cushion. Truly it was the nicest cushion in the house. It had her name on it.

Sadie it read, in beautiful letters. Like a scroll.

He snatched it up.

Her eyes were like a cat's backed into a corner.

"Ahh," she said.

He threw the cushion down and wiped his feet on it, and booted it through the door. He began to upset her books—all Harlequin romances, which were stacked from top to bottom.

"My books—my books."

"Ahh," he said.

"She tried to clutch her books," he told Randy later. "That is the worst of it. Tried to grab onto her books, so I wouldn't hurt them. And that made me worse—I started to tear them—that's the worst part."

Harry stood in the doorway. Arnold glared at him, and he didn't dare enter.

"I'll tear all your books," Arnold said. Harry poked his head into the room, but his head disappeared when Arnold glared at him.

"Where's Gogi Grant!"

"Ahhh," said Sadie, like a true Highlander. She came at him with her teeth, and bit into his arm until blood came.

"Ahh," she said, as blood came out of his elbow.

"So—a little blood," he said, but being infuriated he began to bounce her up and down. She clawed his face, and left a welt under the eye.

The fight was almost over. Yet she struggled on. He wanted to throw her through the window—but couldn't bring himself to do it. The record fell from under her dress and smashed in four pieces, like the four corners of the earth.

He stared at it.

She stared at it.

"You," she said.

"That's Mom's 'Wayward Wind'," he said.

"You broke it," she said immediately. "You did—you

broke it—Mabel," she yelled, "he broke it—he broke it."

She began to claw him again.

"Ahh," he said.

"You broke it—and my books, my books, you tore them—you tore them, you broke my cushion—my only decent cushion."

She glared at the floor. And then sat on her bed, and fumbled with her fingers.

It was horrible.

He could cut his guts open again and let the life drip out of him.

He went downstairs. Mabel sat in the dark and he joined her. Harry came downstairs and sat in the dark also.

Randy came home and said:

"What's everyone sitting in the dark for?"

But he sat down in the dark also. The house was beginning to smell of oil again. It would make you sick with its smell this winter, and in the spring—God in the spring, the flood would come through the walls. Everything was just starting.

After a little while Sadie herself came downstairs, holding her cushion. She sat down and kept smoothing her cushion with her knotty fingers.

"I am not a religious person, not like Harry," she said. "But I know mean people."

"Shut up," Mabel pleaded.

"That's why his girl left him—that's why."

"Shut up—"

"That's why she had an abortion."

"You promised not to tell," Mabel said.

"What do you say?"

Sadie's eyes glittered.

"That's why—she knew—that's why she had an abortion."

After a while the red ribbon she wore in her hair was the only thing visible in the room.

CHAPTER 10

No-one wanted to speak with him—or discuss anything about it. Everyone seemed to support Trenda's decision and he was left out in the cold. Eventually he came to believe that it was for the best. What peace of mind was there in thinking any other way? Except one thing that registered on him like a black tattoo.

She wanted to get pregnant. No-one discussed it with him. Mabel and Sadie and Harry had no reason to. Norman said nothing. So he began talking to himself—just as before.

"She had wanted it."

"So—she must have changed her mind."

"Yes—"

And that was it. Who could say more than that.

"So—she must have changed her mind."

For that's what simplicity dictated.

And it was left at that. It was up to Arnold to ask himself questions. But he was fooled by himself.

Perhaps he was cruel to her.

Perhaps she was forced into making a decision.

"So—she must have changed her mind," he said. And tried to forget it.

A cold wind came in October, and froze the ground. Deer tracks were in the far fields at dawn. Snow fell at the brightest hour of the day, when the sun was high, and neither pebbles nor boulders moved. The cold increased as the minutes passed. On walls the flies stayed still or dropped to doom, the smell of apples in the quiet rooms.

He sat in his room one afternoon. It was bare and small. Gone were the feelings of heat—the summer days. A tube of dye lay cold upon his table. Dust was still, and collected in little balls upon the floor. Cold drafts seemed to make little snatches of conversation about his ears.

In the next room, Sadie sat the afternoon out, and

snatches of conversation went about her ears also.

"Who knows why women do these things."

"She is a spirit all her own that Trenda."

"Who knows why she sat on my knee."

"And then ran away."

"Who knows why?"

"Who suffers more than women?"

"Who knows—"

"Who suffers more than women at eighteen—little women—little women at eighteen."

"I don't know—"

"Who finds her own way is a good spirit."

"A social worker is an evil thing—who comes in the morning and stays till dark."

He could hear Sadie breathing. This house was wounded, and everything was heard.

Only Randy said:

"Seaweed—excuse me, Arnold, is in his bedroom muttering complaints."

Again no-one could bring themselves to speak to him. Mabel looked away, and Sadie didn't answer.

One evening at supper-time, a strange theory was discussed.

"There he is—the man who beat me up," Sadie said.

"Shut up."

"Beat my head off."

"Shut up—oh you shut up," Mabel said.

It was at supper hour—at six o'clock. It was already dark. There was silence for a little moment. Enough to make the pea soup cool.

"We are all nothing anyway," Seaweed said.

"Don't say that," Mabel answered.

"Nothing but dirt—even Harry."

Harry looked offended.

"Shut up," Sadie said.

"Nothing."

"Shut up."

"Yes," Sadie said, "shut up about it!"

She coughed in her soup. The night was already black.

Mabel said:

"Arnold—don't believe—don't believe that—it is awful—"

Arnold neither breathed nor answered.

"Lies are nothing—even Harry is nothing," he said.

"For we are lies—and liars are nothing—they'll be forgotten."

CHAPTER 11

He spoke to Randy. Randy was the only one who seemed willing to listen. Arnold's head was spinning, one afternoon, spinning like his cruel red hair that sat upon him like an Irish town mop. Like inflamed seaweed.

"Randy—Trenda was a tramp I must admit—"

Randy sniffed.

"But she had her way to get around me—so whatever I did to lose her I'm sorry."

"Maybe—it's because of how we act."

They sat in the field. And the tips of the grasses were orange and the day seemed to roll over the hills and naked river.

"One day we were going to have a house—like Matheson's—with a duck pond."

"You were."

"That's one thing I thought we'd have—a duck pond."

Of course he knew that wasn't true. He was just talking. The cold had come to sting his legs. It had come to make the oil barrel cold and the houses look red. It had come to lie flat against the road and wither the cow dung, and make the ferns go black, and make the moths cloud against lights in the dark. It had come to be true. It had come to silence everything.

They sat outside. Anyone who lived here and looked at Randy could tell. They could tell he took the bus to school, and wore his cub sweater until it smelled, and had black wrists.

His brother was sure Randy, with his perplexed look, wanted to help out. Wanted to help Sadie. Wanted to be friends with Juliet, who asked him questions about things he had no idea about or control over. But Randy wanted to help her out. He wanted to cook spinach, to get his housekeeping badge. He wanted to go into the woods with Craig, the cubmaster.

The day was like a broken ankle. Randy stared at the back of the house. Every tree had suddenly turned old and hungry.

"Is everything all right with you?" Arnold asked.

Randy looked toward the house. He breathed quietly. A few hairs stuck up at the back of his head, and Arnold wetted his fingers and pasted them down.

The cop looks at me once again, and tries to be friendly.

Do you lose your temper? he asks me.

Not often.

Once in a while.

Yes.

Is that why you were carrying a rock in your pocket?

Yes.

That's a weapon like everything else.

And this is Canada, and I'm on welfare, I say, so what.

Is that who you blame—Canada.

Sure, why not—

What about you—didn't you go to school?

A teacher picked on me.

He smiled tolerantly. I sit in the swivel chair. Really, I shouldn't have gotten the tattoo on my back. Because now I'm on the open market to be looked at, picked up and questioned. Already the air smells of smoke and dead leaves and cold bones. I don't know what I've got against this fellow—but he makes me itchy.

Do you think your girlfriend is headed down a bad road he asks.

There's not too many roads worse than this I say.

66

Besides, I say, she is not my girlfriend anymore, I
threw her out.
Physically.
As a matter of course.
She goes with Jerry Bines does she?
Does she?
The officer tries to be pleasant—he tries to confide.
I look away, and my lips twitch.
He says:
She's picked a bad one.
He says:
Maybe you're better off without her.
I say:
Go to hell.
He shrugs and lets me go—
To hell if that's the case.

CHAPTER 12

The chimney smoke was in the air. But the fires came
from Canada's cold. There was its passion, which itches
the legs of teenagers.

Arnold had to know this. What he knew the road told
him.

The gardens lay trampled under the bright skies, each
garden an end in itself.

Billy the priest was an alcoholic.

Leaves fell near the road, near the prison site and
across the face of the wet church windows.

Each day was like a broken ankle.

Arnold awoke in the night, sweating, when the full
moon was in the sky. How the earth looked eerie, and
silent, the corn stalks picked over and emptied.

Randy slept beside him, curled up in a small ball. His
cub hat was under the bed, upside down, like a teacup.

The moon played upon it. Arnold's pea-green pants were hanging over the door, like the pants of a criminal.

He put them on and went downstairs. Everything was normal—that is, there wasn't anything to be downstairs for. He felt anger.

Did others have this anger?

Did the rest of creation share his burn?

Or was it just him?

Arnold?

He couldn't tell. How sweet the night was. How tender this autumn—even under the blood-red famished afternoons. There was a stillness everywhere. He thought of how these afternoons were given to him to enjoy, how the little stream that flowed here sparkled, and there was no other way to say this, like diamonds. Clear as cut glass, and rolled-over coloured stones to the river.

I want out.

He thought: I want to get away.

But he had no idea where to go.

He went outside and followed the gravel drive down to the road, bent over and kissed it.

He went to see Billy the priest.

This happened on a cool morning, with black ice in the ditches. He walked to the church. The priest was busy putting on his storm-windows.

Here the river bent and swept away. Salmon lay under the dark water, and red leaves, fallen from maple trees, floated upon it.

"Can you tell me what I should do?" Arnold asked, after he explained that he was unhappy.

The priest told him that he knew many people who were.

Arnold said that this might be true.

"Yes—many people feel this way."

"But one must be true to oneself—and in this way—find God."

Arnold felt ashamed at the word "God."

"And in this way find God."

The priest said.

He smiled.

"You see—that's all anyone is searching for—"

The priest talked longer. He seemed quite animated. Everything he said had a special meaning to him—and Arnold remained polite. The priest said that ignorance was the hateful sin; and that from the teachings, not only of his church, but of society at large—and teachings too, from the very people who thought they knew the most, people were taught to remain ignorant and have a low esteem. This was what he said.

After the priest said this he made Arnold a cup of tea —quite weak by Arnold's standards.

"One must have humility—but of the right kind. False humility is boastful and filled with pride."

"Forgive," the priest said, "then your unhappiness will go away."

He smiled. He looked sad, his face as flat as his kitchen clock.

Arnold smiled. When he smiled, the very top of his red hair seemed to crinkle. But he didn't understand a thing, and no-one explained it to him.

The priest drank his tea, and stared into his cup.

"Yes," the priest said, "forgive, and then your unhappiness will go away."

And now the horrors started, just as before. For instance, he had nervous twitches—but everyone told him nervous twitches made him look mature.

And certain things happened at home that made him slightly morbid.

Randy—who had tried so hard to please Craig, flunked his World Conservation badge. He had flunked other badges also. These badges were the most important things in his life—in fact he became demented at the mere mention of badges.

He had flunked his swimming badge.

His directions badge.

And though Craig had allowed him his housekeeping badge, for cooking spinach, he still needed one more to get into the woods. Some nights Randy would talk in his sleep about badges.

"Did Craig make passing them so difficult?" he asked.

"They aren't so difficult—for normal boys," Craig said.

This made Randy sit on the doorstep with his hands upon his ears, his knees hauled up and the first sign of hatred on his face.

Thus it was generally tense when Randy walked home from cubs.

Why was Craig cubmaster?

Arnold wanted to know. For there was something mean-spirited about him. Yes. But who could he tell?

No-one wanted to know.

Who cared why Craig became cubmaster.

The road knew.

The road told him everything.

The cubs traipsed along behind Craig, who carried a staff.

They were called the Beaver pack.

Randy was the last one, traipsing behind the rest.

He looked like an amphibian in a cub cap.

Randy loved Craig. You could tell. It was easy enough to understand.

There must have been something about Randy that reminded Craig of his own self-indulgent childhood. For he gave the boy a dry, contemptuous look, and often sent him home from the Beaver den, lonely and crying.

Is this what cubs are? Arnold asked himself.

And the answer came from the roadway. Yes.

CHAPTER 13

Juliet stands at my bedroom door. She sees my filthy underwear hanging around. She looks upon this as a normal thing, I think. I must follow her downstairs.

70

Actually, it would be better if we got along. I know of no reason to get along with her however.

"What do you want now?" I ask. I have a surly mouth on me—a mouth with too many germs in it, a nose that smells things she doesn't have to smell.

"Your mom tells me you've been talking about getting a job—"

"So I have," I say.

"Well, do you have any prospects?"

"Ha."

She doesn't answer.

"Ha."

She doesn't answer.

"Maybe—maybe not."

She cleans specks from her glasses with a practised hand.

"Well—what can you do for me?"

"Can't you do things for yourself?"

"Most definitely—"

"Well, don't sit here like a lug—get up—get moving."

I am upset. Almost everyone can tell you that. I keep thinking.

"If a person was going to be murdered would you help them?"

"I don't know what you're talking about—"

I shut up.

She looks at me, and I lose my train of thought. Why does she have to look at the holes in my walls?

"The cops shouldn't question me about things I don't know," I say, "it leads to bad feelings."

"Does it now?"

"Yes, it does," I say, "it leads to all sorts of complications, all kinds of trouble."

I stay in bed all day.

It's common talk that our family is simpleminded.

A lot of people have done away with themselves for less than this. So I feel sorry for myself. I try to forget things, so I won't lie when I say I don't know about them.

Jerry can look at a person as if they are as common-

71

place as a fly, and smile when he does.

One person should shut up, so they won't start trouble for someone else.

It was in the morning when he thought of it.

So he asked her to help him get his teeth fixed. Juliet didn't reply at once, and seemed to be embarrassed.

He looked at her. At first she smiled, but then she became sad. Her glasses were perched on her face and left a red mark on her nose.

"Arnold," she said, "why do you do this—?"

"I don't know why I do it."

"Why didn't you go to the dentist years ago?"

"Oh," he said.

He said this as if he had no idea he had to go to the dentist. But any office such as theirs made you wait. He sat in corners and stared at people. But they made him wait. And when they did look at him he'd look away. So he did not visit places very often. And whenever he had visited them they had just sent him home once more.

She spoke calmly, and told him she couldn't help him.

"Oh," he said. He glanced toward her, and then buried his eyes into her left foot.

She was making him suffer.

He chose not to look at her.

"My teeth aren't very important—they're just a mistake," he laughed, "that's why they keep falling out."

"They've cut back on people's teeth," she said.

"I suppose they had to," he said.

He had no idea what she was talking about. That is, that the province was short of money, and could no longer afford to pay for his teeth.

For years he never cared if they did. The blacker the better. But now he was caught because he had asked her for a favour. She breathed through her nose as if she knew everything about him. She knew everything about Mabel.

She knew all about Randy. (For instance, his bum was chafed. And she knew it all. All about his bum. But

72

Randy knew nothing about her.)

And now Seaweed too. Even Seaweed was asking her favours!

He went upstairs. He sat down on his bed and put his head in his hands. His chest shook and shuddered. And he coughed, and spit in a shoebox under the bed. And that evening he was angry. He was beside himself. So he wasn't thinking clearly again. Things were bad all over. He said:

"Randy you should quit the cubs," and smiled.

"Of course Randy should quit—he should quit cubs," Harry said. "We never had cubs when I was a boy."

"Never had," Arnold sniffed. He was conscious that he sniffed just like his old schoolteacher. It pierced his heart.

Randy's eyes began to water. He looked about for a friend.

"Randy isn't so tough," Sadie said. "He flunked his badges."

"Yes."

"Randy isn't so tough," Harry said, "he'll never get into the woods."

"I will so."

"No you won't—you won't get into the woods—you'll never pass your badges—and if you do, Mabel won't allow you to go."

"She will so."

"I don't know what I'll do," Mabel said. "I haven't made up my mind."

"Well you can't let him go into the woods."

"Leave me alone," Randy said.

He jumped up from the table. They were having beans with pork fat.

"Finish those beans," Mabel yelled.

"It costs good money," Harry said.

Everything smelled of oil and bad weather.

There was bad weather in their hearts.

"I try," Mabel yelled, "I do what Juliet says—I try, I try."

73

"I'll give a few drinks of soapy water," Sadie said.

"You won't," Arnold said. "Or I'll give you a few drinks."

"There's the man—there's the man that beat me up—that beat my head off—that tore my books and bounced me up and down."

"You won't give him any water," Arnold said.

"Leave Mommy be," Harry said.

Then Harry left the kitchen.

A kitchen that smelled.

That had orders from the Department of Social Services tacked on the wall.

Randy slunk away. As skinny as a pretzel.

"There's the man," Sadie said.

Arnold said nothing.

"There's the man—who made his girlfriend cry—

"Who hates his mother.

"Who stabbed himself."

"Who told you!" Arnold said.

"I see the scar."

"You'd better not mess with me."

"I see the scar."

"You'd better not mess with me—I'm Arnold."

"That's why Trenda had an abortion."

"Stop it," Mabel cried.

Mabel held onto her stomach.

"She didn't want to produce another Arnold," Sadie said.

Sadie said:

"Everyone told her—don't produce another Arnold."

"No more Arnolds. Ever again in the history of the world!"

Sadie yawned and took a mouthful of beans.

She was at her best, chewing beans. For she had fought all her life and had good experience in waging battle. She knew as well as most, and she never gave any quarter.

Arnold was crying.

"Look at the tears," Sadie said.

"Crocodile tears."

74

"Just like every other man."

Sadie said:

"Good for Trenda—good for her."

(There was a fight at the house. One of those terrible things that happen without anyone knowing why. It started as they all did—as every other fight in the world started at the house, with no-one to blame. It was a bad night, a night when everything goes wrong without anyone doing much to make it so. And then, after the dishes were broken—for they were broken—and after the kitchen became a stink hole of burnt meat, for the frying-pan was left on in the midst of the trouble, and after Randy was bruised on both arms by someone twisting them—though no-one would admit to it—and after all the insults and cruel remarks whipped everyone into hatred—a hatred that is almost like happiness because of the rage that descends over their heads, Juliet stood in the midst of them, trying to restore order. It was so awful for them to see her holding out her hands in a peaceful way, and trying to placate them, that no-one could stomach her. For no-one believed, least of all themselves, that she could do anything. But he looked upon her, as she came through the back door, beyond the stinking garbage pots, and held her hands aloft, as if to offer them peace.

Yet especially now, he glared at her, and was joined by the others. For all of them felt like betraying her. And without even thinking, someone hit her in the face.

"Ohh," she said, putting her hands over her nose.

Her pink glasses, thick and ugly, hung by one small ear.

"Look," Sadie said, "look what Arnold did—"

"I didn't," Arnold said. "It wasn't me."

But they seemed to all want to blame him.

"Why don't you get the hell away from us," Mabel screeched at him.

"I didn't hit her—it wasn't me." Arnold answered.

Juliet, a little bit of blood running to her chin, her eyes closed in pain, had driven all this way to tell him he had another job interview. Now, instead, blood stained the top of her blouse, her hands were trembling and her mouth was wet.

Arnold got a facecloth and held it over her nose. He held it there for the longest time, certain that if he applied pressure all the pain and blood would go away.)

CHAPTER 14

They knew the cold so well that they had a passion for it, and crawled inside it for its beating heart.

The prison now and then reared its cold head above the trees far off.

A certain plane had sprayed the trees last summer and had killed the birds. Randy and he had watched it for many days. Though now they watched nothing but the air as cold as liquid descending upon them.

"Why are they building the prison here?" Arnold asked Norman one afternoon.

"Because they are," Norman said.

"Oh well, we'll work there soon enough," Arnold said.

He tried to comfort Norman with this. How could a man like Norman not work? It was all right for some people, and there was no shame in it if a person so decided.

"Oh well, you'll work there soon enough," Arnold said.

It was a good day to smell the air and to know that lies had a cold walk in order to reach you. They must traverse a long way over many a frozen field and small dead gullies, past leaves that had begun to fall against the side of shale cliffs, and many a frozen windfall.

Norman spit at the mention of the prison.

"Sooner or later a man with no work might be inside a prison—everything points to it," Arnold said, under his breath.

Norman's eyes burned. His eyes moved as if he was

quickly trying to sight on something, and his hair was as coarse as gravel. The top of his arms burned with tattoos that he hid from people. He said nothing.

"Norman," Arnold said. "I know you didn't rob my mother. It must have been someone else."

Norman watched him uneasily.

Norman would return to his house.

That looked like a shoebox, with a flat roof and a poked hole to allow a stove-pipe; and the picture of a big-eared dog, which he had bought for his wife the night she left him.

His wife had red hair, pumpkin-coloured. His wife had red hair, pumpkin-coloured hair, and they lived in a house shaped like a shoebox. His wife had pumpkin-coloured hair.

Everyday Norman cleaned the house, swept the floor and polished the oil cloth. The two windows he cleaned looked in two directions.

But now he was alone, and what else was there to say?

"Trenda robbed your mother," Norman said.

Arnold was silent.

"Jerry robbed your mother. In fact they wanted me to help."

Arnold stood and walked away. The back of his head trembled.

"That's why she hates me," Norman continued, "because I wouldn't help her."

"Everyone knows Norman—you don't like women."

Norman said nothing. For if you tell the truth and no-one listens what else can you do?

Arnold was twitching. He was filled with anger and shame, as if he'd long been angry and shameful. (As a matter of fact he couldn't remember when he hadn't been.)

"You're no friend of mine," he said. "Everyone knows —why, you hit your wife with a ketchup bottle, everyone knows. Why, ask Sadie—Sadie will tell you. You walloped your wife with a ketchup bottle."

Norman said:

77

"I will tell you Jerry and Trenda robbed your mother!"

"Everyone knows, Norman, you don't like Jerry. But Jerry Bines is good people—a lot of people don't think too well of him but he's always been good to me."

Norman remained still.

"Do you think the social workers care for you—they don't care if you starve, but they care for me—they care for my house."

Arnold spoke.

Norman didn't speak.

Arnold said all this in eight seconds. And it seemed as if a lie had travelled throughout him, and his body ached from the boots up, and his head was heavy.

Norman stared at the ground.

Arnold lit a cigarette. And blew the match out in a split second. He exhaled smoke something like a cowboy, and was furious with himself.

Sadie listened out her upstairs window.

Harry stood still in the backyard.

Mabel stared at the *National Enquirer*.

Randy was in school.

'You think you're too good for Sadie," Arnold said.

He went over and poked Norman with a stick.

"Hey you—you think you're better than poor old Sadie!"

He couldn't stop poking Norman with the stick—it was the worst feeling he'd ever had.

CHAPTER 15

The cold was like a sharp bone in the flesh. The girls waited for the school bus under the grey beginning.

Randy, too, went to school.

Arnold stared out the blank window.

Sadie sat in the upstairs room.

Cold passed over the ground and hung like a drape over the house. The yard lay thick as tongues.

Randy's bicycle, with its plastic flags, lay like a dead animal in the dirt. Across the river there was a billboard with the picture of the girl, lying on blue cloud, in blue jeans, who had had her private parts written over in paint, by youngsters on Hallowe'en.

Everything was still.

And then one day the road collapsed.

It sunk in, rolled over and fell away. People came out of the doors of their houses to look at it.

"God's mad," Sadie said.

"The road rotted away," Mr. Matheson said.

Everyone nodded. How could a road rot away? No-one cared to ask. It just did. It rotted away without saying a thing—without groaning it rotted, and after it rotted, it fell away in front of their eyes.

Or as they said, it was the last shift of earth beneath it —before the winter set in for eight months.

Even the TV showed a picture of it, from an airplane.

So without searching, without trying for a job, Arnold found a job fifteen yards from his doorstep.

Sometimes fate works its hand. For he hadn't searched along the roadway for fifteen months as Norman had. Nor did Norman find a job here—though he could have worked at anything they gave him. He was as strong as two men.

Arnold couldn't question this, or allow himself to think of it.

Norman hadn't been seen since Arnold had poked at him with the stick. He hadn't gotten off his cot in the back-room of his house.

He had become a recluse.

And so, he had missed his one opportunity at work. A stinking job though it was.

Arnold was given the job. He had to stand in the middle of the highway—from dark in the morning until evening, and direct traffic around the hole that was there. The oil lanterns burned, black smoke rose in the calm afternoons, the earth fell prey to quick snow and frost and early dark.

Conversations were heard far away, and overheard.

Arnold wore an orange hunting-vest, and earmuffs to cover his ears. Each morning he stood in the same spot.

When a car came along he would wave to it.

"When are they coming to fix it?"

"Tomorrow," Arnold said.

Everyday.

When are they coming to fix it.

"Tomorrow."

And so it went.

But no-one came, and no-one mentioned it.

It was evil, to have the road out. Everyone knew it was.

One dirty morning a man named Donnie went off the road and hit the sewer pipe. He came up out of the ditch, covered with snow.

"Look," he said, "I should kick your head in."

And he threatened Arnold with a tire iron.

Other than this the days passed like a beating heart. The snow stayed, though the fields were still half-bare, and twigs and bits of bark showed their cold faces. The boys walked the road late in the afternoon. Sometimes Arnold would overhear conversations.

And distant machinery whining.

And smell cold gasoline.

One day, close to dark he heard three boys talking.

"Norman has given up," they said. "He won't be here next year, he'll move away!"

Arnold hadn't remembered Norman giving up before. Even after his wife went away.

His wife had pumpkin-coloured hair.

Hair like a pumpkin, and smooth as silk.

But even then Norman stood against the wall.

He didn't even say his wife had lied or had accused him falsely.

He hadn't once tried to protect himself. And Arnold knew that when he poked him with a stick he did the worst thing possible.

Arnold said:

"I will go to see him and tell him I'm sorry."

But then he thought:

"No, let him come to me!"

And these were his thoughts.

In November, a truck and a tractor, a grader and twelve men came one morning. They came from the south of the province, and they came for seventeen days. They stayed in the motel in town, and complained. They complained about the people:

"The people over north," they said.

Arnold said nothing to them, and they asked him questions.

Perhaps what they found the most amusing was his accent.

"Say 'Good afternoon' for us again."

"Good afternoon for us again," Arnold would say.

And their shouts of laughter could be heard everywhere.

Especially, when in a weak moment, he admitted that he had a nickname.

"What's your nickname?"

"Seaweed."

One of them seemed to have been kicked in the head, for he rolled on the ground holding it.

They asked him questions all afternoon. Then they went away laughing, and quarrelling with one another. Arnold never asked them any questions. He never asked why they came here, instead of having people from here working. Because he didn't want to be rude.

The next day they asked him questions again.

And the next.

"Do you have a girlfriend?"

"I have a girl—only we don't see each other no more— because she's taken up with someone else."

Two of the men jabbed each other in the ribs, as if this was a thing to be joked about. He saw that they were doing this, but still he thought: "It's a thing people do."

"Why don't you see each other anymore Seaweed?"

"She went away," he said, and in a moment added, "she was too good for me."

While some laughed, others said nothing.

One, a student, who was working a year before he went back to university, said:

"I can't imagine that."

Arnold said nothing.

"Seaweed—did she wear panties?"

This brought hoots of laughter. He tried to smile, and hold his sign erect.

Their lips were cracked from the cold and the ground was as solid as death. The highway stretched away.

"What's the name of this place?"

Though they knew the name well enough.

Arnold said nothing.

"Did she wear panties Arnold?" one of the men said.

But after that they said nothing for a while.

When Randy got off the school bus Arnold hoped that he wouldn't come over.

He held his sign erect and straightened up, but when Randy walked over he stared at his boots.

Randy's hands were raw, and his nose was starting to run.

Arnold look at him.

He felt guilty once more.

"Hi Arnold."

"Hi."

"Directin' traffic?"

"Not much traffic to direct."

"Got yer lanterns goin'?"

"Yes."

"I can see ya way off in that orange jacket."

"Yes."

"I can see ya-all the way down there."

"Go home."

"What?"

"Go home—go on home—"

Randy looked at him.

He wouldn't look at his brother. He kept looking here

and there. He thought the men were all waiting to start something.

"I thought I'd keep ya company."

"I don't want your company—"

"Gotcher long underwear on."

"Go home."

Randy picked his nose. Arnold couldn't look at anyone.

Randy looked up at him. Wearing one of those polyester winter jackets he looked like a saint in a spacesuit. And Arnold thought: "Why doesn't he get the hell out of here."

"Want what's left over in my lunch?"

"No."

"Do the men—maybe the men want what's left over in my lunch—I have a peanut-butter sandwich—left over in my lunch."

"They don't want to eat your fucking lunch—go home."

Randy stepped away. He took two steps back.

"I'll just set my lunch bucket here," he said. He backed away.

The rest of the evening that crazy bucket with the picture of Goofy and Pluto looked at Arnold, and sized him up.

It sized him up too well.

Sadie knew it.

She said:

"Imagine the likes of some people working when even Norman can't get work."

It was as bad in the house as ever, even worse.

"Poor Norman," Sadie said, "I always had a soft spot for Norman."

"Yes," Mabel said.

"Perhaps if a man gets a job, he should move away, and leave others in peace—"

There was nothing more to do. But to wait for the snow.

He, like everyone, waited for the snow, longed for it

like a half-sick animal. And he couldn't tell you any different.

He couldn't say:

"I hate the snow," as the student did.

Because he longed for it. So it must be. He waited for it to cover the black branches like piled bones. He waited for it when the sun was at its brightest and showed his house for what it was, and crept over the ancient brick pump-house with half the bricks blackened.

Sadie sat in the room.

Mabel read *True Confessions.*

The TV burned in the living-room, and in the middle of the day, after the game show, showed them sun, and skin-diving.

But they turned away from it.

They turned their heads away, and stared out the window. The black oil lanterns burned.

The student complained. He complained and let dark sighs come from his compressed lips.

"I am not made for this," he said, prancing on his feet to keep warm.

"I am made for warmer climates than this and talk, and good food, and restaurants."

Arnold said nothing. Nor did the men. They said nothing, for they hadn't the vocabulary of the student.

"Look," the student said. He pointed to the naked river, the hills half eaten by machinery, the towers of the prison and the stark land like bruised skin. "Who was made for this?"

Arnold smelled the air. He sniffed it through his half-closed nostrils.

"Look," the student said, "how could they have decided to live here? What possessed them?"

He dug at the road like a joyless dog. But no-one answered him.

Arnold said nothing.

"Anywhere man might think of could be better than this," said the student.

He was really bundled up. He was so bundled he

squeaked when he walked.

His boots made squeaking noises.

Arnold found out about the student. The student had flunked his second year of law, and couldn't practise, and his family was upset. One of the men told Arnold this at dinner-hour one afternoon. So Arnold knew. He said to himself:

"A real lawyer—almost—"

Here he cut his thoughts short. It had begun to snow, and snow as pleasantly as he remembered when he was a child at Christmas. Big white flakes floated to the ground and the earth once again smelled of holly and evergreen.

"Well—there's snow anyway."

But the student went on complaining. He did not sniff the air.

"Welfare," he said. He looked like he could spit. "No-one has enough shame to work."

Everyone was silent.

"I'll get a job at the prison," Arnold said.

"Yes I'm sure."

"I could get a job and feed my family."

"What family?"

Everyone laughed.

"Randy," Arnold said, "I could feed and clothe Randy."

"You'd do better to get your fucking teeth fixed," the student said, wiping his mouth quickly.

Everyone laughed.

So Arnold said nothing.

He felt the blood in his heart. He sniffed the dirt and gravel.

It's terrible who you admit things to. And the worst things about yourself.

The student sat on the sewer pipe one day blowing his nose, and Arnold thought:

"He really has the smallest feet I've ever seen on a grown man."

When the student saw him watching, he looked away, insulted.

Arnold crossed the ditch and sat beside him. For some reason he began to tell things about his life, how he grew up and what he thought about. Then he talked about Trenda. He told the student how he met her and what she meant to him and all she said and did. Then he told him about the night she left in September, and how he had broken his good-luck feather. He trembled all over as he spoke. He talked about his trip to town and how they ran from him. He told about his guilt over getting this job when Norman lay upon his cot, a recluse. It seemed to come out of him like water—pour from him.

And he had no idea why.

After he was finished the student was smiling slightly.

Arnold straightened his earmuffs.

He said nothing more.

He tried not to look at the student, realizing he'd made an awful confession. The student stared across the river saying nothing at all. His wispy beard, which was frozen, seemed to crinkle. Whatever he had told the student, who had a beard like all students and eyes like most students, and whose nose was red, seemed to please him. It suddenly seemed as if the student were thinking:

"I could have messed myself up like that—but I haven't."

This is what it seemed like.

The student walked back to the men, his boots squeaking.

And do you think the student could keep his mouth shut about everything?

That confession was really like hell on earth.

But Arnold kept thinking.

"If Stephen bothers me again I'll get even."

That was the student's name. Stephen.

Arnold knew how people treated people. So why did he confess such things—such ordinary everyday things? His sins.

Because what he had told the student was soon all they talked about.

The student kept them at it.

"Do you know what Seaweed had?"

"No—what in the world did Seaweed have?"

"A good-luck—feather."

Arnold went home.

His eyes looked more determined than ever. Even Sadie kept her distance. He sat in the big chair at his own leisure and stared at the road, the oil lanterns burning away like bodies, and he thought:

"I am Arnold—"

As little bodies of smoke came from the blackening road, he said:

"He'll not talk about me again."

"What's that?" Harry said.

"Ha," Arnold said.

The next day he carried a black rock in his pocket. With the crease the earmuff wire made, his red hair looked like it had been shot at. From a distance.

He waited in vain for the student to say something.

But Stephen was in a quiet mood. In fact no-one bothered with him. But Arnold was bothered. He sniffed the tormented sky.

And felt blood in his eardrums. And padded about in the dry white snow.

So he asked them:

"Who wants a rock over the side of their head?"

They looked at him and said nothing.

"You think about it," he said.

"What are you talking about?"

"You think about it—all of you," he said. And he pulled the rock from his pocket and showed it to them. He smiled quickly, and the blood seemed to stay in his head. He sniffed the air and let out a low howl.

"What's troubling you?" one of them asked.

But he simply howled in a low tone for an hour or more.

And tossed the rock from one hand to the other.

CHAPTER 16

Sadie coughs all night and in the morning I see her. She is an old woman.

There is no doubt about it.

Nothing can be done for her.

Mabel is playing Christmas music, and getting out the box of Christmas decorations and looking at them—at Christmas cards yellowed from years at the bottom of a box. I see her also. Once she was not a bad-looking woman, my mother.

They have fired me from the road, and I spend most of my time sitting on the stair steps, so I won't have to look out a window and see them. Sadie says:

"My, they're fine workers."

She walks about the house talking about all the workers she knew when she was a girl. Workers in the woods, workers in the fields, workers on the water. Workers who went to war and died in some hole in Europe, or were handcuffed and shackled on the beaches of Dieppe— Canadians, looked upon as barbarians by almost everyone. These are the old stories. We have to understand them. No-one here does. My family has forgotten so much about it by now.

One night Mabel tells me she is sorry I never grew any bigger.

It doesn't matter.

I'm sorry you never grew. I closed all the drapes when you were a child, so you could sleep—and I prayed for you. People do a lot of growing when they sleep.

I don't answer.

I prayed that you'd grow.

Thank you very much.

Who knows, this might be our last Christmas together.

And so what if it is?

But I know I have offended her.

Anyway Christmas has never been so special here. People always complained about what they got.

Somebody always got something more.
Our wood stove used to stink.
And now our oil one smells of oil.
No, I'm not particularly fond of Christmas. I think it comes with going road-looking, and seeing all the decorations out in the other houses, and knowing people were as comfortable as could be, and then to come home to your own house, with the smell of ice and water.
But that's what my mother could give me.
I suddenly realize this.
She could give me nothing else.
Sadie coughs, and tells a dirty joke. Harry laughs.
So I go for a walk.
Only we know the cold.
I am convinced of this more than I am convinced of anything else. The snow has already fallen on the dead-end, on all the walkways, on all the trampled leaves. It has fallen against all God's silent dumpheaps across the river, where smoulder a thousand forgotten utensils, and dreams. It falls on the iron porch-railings that already glitter with their Noels, on all things endless and beginning.
This is what I think. I think it very quickly so I can never tell you what I mean.
I can never tell you why I got the tattoo on my back.
I never know why I smell gritty stove dirt in my blood, or why I falsely told the RCMP officer I blamed Canada for my own lost mistakes.
Trenda stops me in the middle of the road now. The snow glitters in the moonlight, and under the moon in a field near a forgotten barn rests a forgotten plough-blade, which belonged to Jerry's grandmother.
Her teeth sparkle when she looks at me. In the last little while she has changed.
The moonlight shines on the black scarf that covers her hair. She is beautiful even in winter, beautiful enough to cause pain.
I wipe my mouth with a bare hand, which in the moon-light sweeps across my face like a yellow bone. My breath

burns away from my mouth in the direction of the prison.

She is wearing a diamond on her finger.

"Jerry is looking for you," she says. "He wants to talk to you—ask you some questions."

"So—is he a cop too?"

"He thinks you have gone to the police about certain things—you know."

I shrug.

"I haven't."

(At one time, I think, she listened to me, and now she wants me to take orders from her. I think this and become ashamed of how I look to her. Nothing at all.)

"I am told to tell you that things are in the past and should be left there—"

I can say nothing.

"I'm to tell you that Jerry Bines is good people."

I blink.

I blink again.

"Good people—and that I'll be Mrs. Jerry Bines—things in the past should be forgotten."

The wind creeps over us and her mouth parts, alert to the wind, and sensual. She hooks one leg slightly so it touches mine, and I feel it trembling. Even in winter her coat is open and her sweater leaves her belly bare, as brown and pudgy as a groundhog's.

"Why do you love me?" she asks.

"Who says I do?"

With the money from the road job he had his teeth fixed.

He had a set of teeth that by any standards weren't much, and made his face look fatter. This produced an anxiety in him. Though he was proud of them he looked different.

"You have your teeth I see," Juliet said. "Well—how do you like them?"

She had come back the morning after her punch in the nose, and had brought extra bedding for the winter. She brought scribblers and pencils for Randy, and a new

Canada Food Guide for Mabel. Everyone felt ashamed of themselves, and worse, no-one would own up to punching her. When they found out that she hadn't mentioned it to anyone, they all hid from each other, trying to forget it one by one.

He sat on the edge of the bed in his room. Christmas was around the corner, the boys played road hockey and Mr. Matheson had decorations in his store, and people were chopping trees behind his house, and carrying them through the back field.

"We must get a tree," he said to Randy.

Randy slept.

Every now and then Arnold would look into the mirror across the room and smile.

Though he was contented now and happy to see the snow, he was bothered by the fact that Trenda and Jerry would be married. Mabel told him this shouldn't bother him. And he took it standing up, standing straight and not clenching his fists.

"We have a marriage in the community," Sadie said.

"A blessed event—a marriage."

When Arnold passed her in the dark corners of the house she would talk about this blessed event.

"They certainly will make a good life for themselves," she said. She chatted away to no-one.

Still, some nights he dreamed all sorts of things.

That she would suddenly realize who she was again. Barring that, he dreamed he'd make a success of himself, and she'd be envious.

But these dreams left him.

And other than two turkeys—one from Father Billy and the other from Juliet—life was much the same. They talked about what they should do with two turkeys, and then decided that the reasonable thing to do would be to keep them both. Then they worried should Father Billy find out about Juliet's turkey or Juliet find out about Father Billy's, and they locked their door.

Other than this, life was much the same. In fact, Randy had become a little bully, and though he was smaller than most of the other cubs, would pick up anything to hit them with when he was angry.

Craig came to see them about it and seemed upset over it.

"Well," Arnold said, "did you know that in the foster home he was beaten by the bigger boys and ordered about?"

"So," Mabel said, "he's just getting even now!"

"Yes," Arnold said, "he's just getting even—that'll teach them."

Craig didn't bother to take his hat off and the flaps hung down over his ears. His boots melted snow on their floor.

But that night they changed their minds. Their minds were mixed up—what with the turkeys and Christmas coming.

"What did you hit that other cub with!" Mabel yelled.

"A stick."

So Mabel didn't know what to do about it, so she slapped him with a belt until her stomach hurt. So that took some of the pain away.

"I hate you," Randy screamed, "I hate you all—fuck you all." He screeched.

"It's for his own good," he thought.

But he had a hard time to catch his breath over one matter and another would begin. Just as soon as he had forgotten one black mood, another would begin.

People should mind their own business.

And stop trying to make cub-scouts out of people.

And truthfully he hated his own ignorance, and dirty jokes told at every meal.

For a while he too began telling them, and he found out that he was the very centre of attention, and got a good laugh from Sadie at the expense of others he'd never seen or known.

Then for some reason he stopped telling them. He refused to tell any more. He refused and wouldn't open his mouth when Mabel asked him:

"Tell us a joke Seaweed."

But he couldn't. He couldn't do it.

And so the jokes were once again circulated without him.

And people ignored him at the supper table once again.

He went for long walks, and brought a tree home to the house. And whenever anyone talked to him he sniffed. He put the tree up and collected enough boughs and made a wreath. And one afternoon he helped Randy build a feeder out of an old coffee can for wintering birds.

So Randy was able to get his World Conservation Badge, and Craig promised him a trip into the woods. They would stay a weekend in the spruce woods between the road and the tracks. Tracks that no train had travelled since 1948.

This, in a way, was his Christmas present to his brother.

He went to town and bought a pack of Harlequin romance novels for Sadie.

He bought Harry a lighter.

He bought his mother a picture book of movie stars.

None of these things were expensive.

"Randy," he said, taking off his boots that night, "loneliness is the human condition."

He lay down and lit a cigarette and let the ashes fall across his belly, as always. The ashes fell against his scar, as before, and left minute red welts.

CHAPTER 17

Ah well, anger returned. Returned to the house, to the remote roadway itself.

Perhaps it was because of the cold, which came so swiftly after Christmas as to insult you. Eight days in a row he had to boil hot water and pour it over the oil line. Yet the oil line froze again and the furnace went dead.

Harry stayed in bed.

And it was as if they were left alone. For who else would come by to see them? The Christmas tree remained standing in the living-room, its branches sticking out into the hallway. But no-one bothered to take it down. It sagged and looked sick.

"Harry," he said, "it's after New Year—you take the tree down."

"You take the tree down yourself."

"You take it down, before all its needles fall out."

"You take it down yourself before its needles fall out."

And the smell of smoke. Of Harry's cigarettes, and his cigarettes, and Mabel's cigarettes and Sadie's filled the house like it would a toilet.

And everyone smoked in the dry rooms, waiting to freeze.

Juliet had gone on vacation. She hadn't stayed here for Christmas, and so had left, and had taken her looks of mistrust with her.

"You will amount to nothing, Harry, lying on that bed," Arnold said.

"You're nothing."

"So are you—a big fat nothing—a big jerk."

"So are you," Harry squeaked.

"So are you," Arnold stabbed back.

"Leave me alone."

"Leave me alone."

"I didn't do nothin'."

"So I see."

All this fighting was bad for his nerves. At the moment this was happening, Mabel was lying in bed with a bottle of aspirin.

Aspirin, that's all she took. Because she had taken it for birth and menstruation. She had taken it always. So aspirin it was.

Nothing could convince her that it didn't heal her wounds. But Arnold walked up the stairs. His flames of

94

red hair shot up and he had his earmuffs on.

"You're not sick," he said to Mabel.

"I am Arnold dear—I am," she said weakly.

"Help me take the tree down."

"Oh Arnold."

"Help me take the tree down."

"Can't you do it?"

"No—I put it up."

She tried to rise from the bed, sat up on one elbow. Look at her fluffy slippers on the floor, he thought. The most ridiculous fluffy pink slippers I've ever come across. As if she needed them.

He left her lying there, but gave her a bad look as if he were hard-pressed.

"What a Christmas this has been," he said in exasperation.

"Arnold please."

"I had to do everything," he said, standing alone in the hallway.

He sat in the living-room, amidst the smell of failure.

"I'd better not fight again," he said.

His body shook. The day passed minute by minute.

Passed, and went away.

Harry.

Sadie.

Mabel.

Randy.

He said this over and over again, wondering what to do.

Craig.

Juliet.

He said their names with his tongue, always watching for the night.

Billy the priest.

"I'm going to get angry," he said.

No-one answered.

They slept away from the cold as best they could.

Alone with their little beds.

"I'll go out and start trouble," he said.

"When?" Harry said.

"Tomorrow—after breakfast—I'll get even."

"With who," Sadie said. She robbed him of his dignity.

"With everyone."

"No-one's done anything to you—you done it to yourself," Sadie said. "Juliet said as much."

Arnold said nothing.

"Juliet has you figured out."

Arnold gritted his teeth, two at a time. They sounded like Sadie's.

"Juliet's gonna take Randy away when she comes back from holiday—and put him in a good home."

"If she does—" Arnold said.

"She will," Sadie said.

"She'll be sorry."

"Ha," Sadie said.

The laugh rose in the cold, a laugh on stilts. Sadie could certainly laugh.

"Please," came the voice from Mabel's room, "don't talk to each other."

"Be quiet," Harry said, "for Mabel's sake."

"Seaweed's downstairs sittin' in the chair," Sadie said. "He thinks he's some good, because he got a Christmas tree—"

"Please," came Mabel's voice.

"He thought she was his woman but she married another man."

She really did have a bad voice—why did she sing?

"I'm not taking it down," Arnold said. "It'll stand there until it rots."

"I'm not taking it down," Sadie sang.

"I'm going out and get even," he said. "When the thaw comes—I'll get Jerry."

"Jerry is a real man—a real man—he's too much of a man for you."

He didn't answer.

"Better man all around. He's married now—did you know?"

For two days he looked out the window in order to get

even. His lips were thin, and his eyes were set. Who would pass by that he might get even with?

"Juliet's away getting a tan," he said. "That's how much she cares for you, Sadie."

Sadie said nothing.

"One should enjoy herself," Harry said.

"We have no oil—it's run out."

"What do you mean, we have no oil?" Harry said.

"Well—we have no oil," Arnold said. "I can't say it clearer than that—I can oblige you only by saying 'we have no oil.'"

"Check the oil Harry dear," Sadie yelled.

"Yes—check the oil," Mabel protested.

Even she would rather believe Harry, he thought.

"Yes Harry—check the oil," he said, "get up and check it—and please everyone."

Harry didn't stir though. Not a muscle. He slept with himself. He had a wife once, that was certain, but she died. Often he'd spoil a meal by telling you how his wife died. He couldn't wait for some other time to tell you.

Ah.

Arnold let his tongue roll over his mouth.

Ahhh.

He walked into the kitchen. Harry had the oven door open.

"He's getting heat down here," Arnold yelled. "He has the oven open."

There was a good heat coming from the electric oven and Harry was smoking a cigarette. He had his feet on the oven door and was reading a book.

Arnold had worn his earmuffs until his ears were numb and he had a pair of gloves on his hands, plus a blanket trailed from his shoulders, and he had his two pairs of pants on, his red ones and his green ones.

"So," he said, "what are you cooking?"

He said it as manly as possible, as cold breath floated out of his mouth in a little stream.

Harry scrambled away from him.

"You're crazy," Harry said. "Momma says you're crazy

97

—you tried to kill yourself."

Sadie came down the stairs; so did Mabel. All of them knew certain things.

"Phone the oil company!" his mother said.

Yet who had a phone?

"No—they aren't going to get me to beg," he said.

"Ha!" Mabel said.

"Ha!" Sadie said.

Everyone hated each other again. Everyone gathered about the oven, pushing each other out of the way.

Everyone stuck in the knife.

Juliet came home again, and got them the oil before the house froze solid. But Arnold took no notice of it and lowered his eyes to the world. Craig slipped into the house and took Arnold aside. He talked to Arnold about responsibility.

"Don't you realize what might have happened in this house?" he said.

He said more than that and bantered on about things that must have been troubling him.

So they had oil once more. The furnace came on and warmed the kitchen, warmed the rude picture window that looked into the dark. And all the stars were out. Arnold tried to think about what Craig said.

"I must take responsibility," he said, "Craig is right!"

Yet just a year ago he would have spit at their feet. He would have spit if he had thought about their feet.

Craig is right.

There isn't anything wrong with him. He hasn't a cold, or a running nose, his lungs are clear and he breathes silently. Dogs wag their tails amid the cold porches, and the night is here. The rabid squalid night of no people is here. The night when, looking for hours out a clear window one car creeps over the gutted landscape, then there are no more, the narrow fields cut to the water like shears, then there is silence, the hockey game is over, then they are shut-ins, already longing for this hour to be gone and winter to be ended, the gravelpits like shotgun blasts in this dark.

The dark, where he can think.

He remembers the look of disdain on their faces when he went to them. Did Judas see this disdain running about the mouths of the attorneys that long-ago night? Who knows such things? He remembers the constable who had questioned him about the knife in his pocket, which was never used on those he had intended it for, looking upon him as God himself must have looked upon the lepers.

They didn't ask him to tell them anything—he just assumed that he was doing right. No, really he assumed no such thing. He just found himself there, in the hot white office on a stiff chair, blinking continually, and rubbing his hands through his hair.

So now he was taking responsibility.

"I might know who killed the Norwegian."

"Tell us about the break-ins at the vault why don't you?"

That was to trick him, to make him unsure of himself.

"Jerry had just moved to town," he said calmly, "he was at my place a lot. He picked on my place because we are neighbours—who would want him there? And one night he brought the Norwegian."

"How do you know it was the Norwegian? It might have been anybody—is Jerry a homosexual?"

"The reason I came here was to tell you what I know." He looked from one to the other and then asked for a cigarette. The pale little office shook when the wind blew, and he edged closer to the heater and made a joke of it. "The man he brought to my apartment was a foreigner—Norwegian. I'm just doing what any citizen should do if he has a clear conscience."

"Is Jerry a homosexual?"

"How would I know—if he is he is—I don't know about such things—I've come to tell you what I know."

"Yes," they said.

The world was crazy. It was better to be on Jerry's side

than theirs. All that was left for him was to leave their office and go home.

"We'll be in touch with you," they told him. "We have a lot of information about Jerry Bines."

"As for the Norwegian—we don't even know if he's dead—he could be hiding out. A lot of people would give their right eyebrow to live in this country."

"He was a pleasant fellow—he wouldn't have hurt a fly," Arnold told them. He smiled nervously, and twitched his little fingers.

It was best to go home, but he had done something wrong and he knew it. He couldn't sleep because of it, and he took to looking out the window. He could have told them about other things. He too had gone into the vault with Jerry and Jerry had given him a watch. It was an easy robbery. He hid it and never did he wear it. Jerry had given him the only watch he'd ever had.

So he forgot to tell about that. He had kept guard that evening while Jerry had broken into it, and had stood there until Jerry came out. Then Jerry gave him the watch and patted him on the back as if they would always be friends. Yet how could you feel close to someone who robbed your mother and walked uncaring across your father's grave?

Everything had changed. It had changed like dirt in the wind.

"The cops are all crooks too," he thought. "It puts me in a bad way."

I caught my mother crying. Her hands busily tried to fix the clock radio, and her tears came down her face. It made me nervous.

This road is in trouble. No-one treats the other with respect. My mother sniffs and her hands tremble as she twists the dial. There are many ways of crying—I know them all.

My mother cries in a way peculiar to us. She cries silently, as if no-one would help her anyway, and her shoulders shake as if they're scared to be seen.

"Get out of here," she tells me.

"I'm sorry I broke your clock radio," I say.

"It doesn't matter."

"I'll get you a new one."

"It doesn't matter—"

"I'm just sick of listening to it."

"It doesn't matter."

"I threw it against the wall before I had a chance to say, 'Ooops.'"

How unmechanical her hands are: like mine. I feel bad about the whole affair. Her hands twist and cling at different parts of the radio, as if just by touching it she can heal its wounds. She brushes the top of it with her fingers, as if to heal it that way, smooth the dents. Its buzzer goes off and makes a peculiar dying sound.

"I've been acting bad lately—I think I'll go away."

She stares at the radio, as one would a dead animal. And her lips are puffy and blue, as if she is suffering deep in her blood, a torment I don't know about. She listened to all the CBC shows on it. She laughed when it told her to laugh, and got upset when it told her to. Each morning the radio was on before anything else, telling her things.

It was her only leverage with others. Even I was surprised that she knew about certain things, and once my mother smiled, as beautiful as I've ever seen her and said:

"I like to keep informed."

Today I threw it against the wall.

I have hit my mother four times in the last month, just so I could feel sorry for her bruised mouth. I have kicked Harry just so I might notice the instant confusion in his eyes, and look away. I have noticed Randy's face, set and hard as a little man's when Juliet talks to him. He has begun to look at her as if she were nothing, even when she brings him warm mitts for his hands, which she has taken the trouble to knit herself.

CHAPTER 18

Two government inspectors came one afternoon.

"Don't you know why Randy's bum is chaffed, and his legs spotted," they said.

"No."

"You have no idea do you?"

"None at all—lice?"

One made a face—imperceptible to anyone who didn't know the faces that those who are right can make toward those who are wrong. The faces that say:

"Yes—your opinion and your life are nothing." So February came with more problems. The bum was the problem. The sun was as hard as granite, and the prison had started again. The machinery sounded clean and quiet. Who could tell by all the excitement this prison had generated in this back end of the province that it was a building of sorrow and horror? No-one in authority wanted to tell them this.

Well, the sound was nice. Sometimes the windows rattled from the wind that came upon you in gusts. The sun shone on the whole room. The little vase Mabel had bought in town with the picture of Charles and Di. The TV with a pint of dust on its top. The picture of the Queen. The tree, not as spry as it used to be, with its two electrical cords unplugged.

"So, what's the problem?" Seaweed said.

They told him. It was a simple problem. The problem for once hadn't even been created by themselves; and even the men's faces showed signs of sympathy and understanding.

Their house was filled with bad insulation. Ureaformaldehyde. Well, what was new?

They sat in the living-room listening to this story.

Didn't the government give them a grant to put in insulation?

Yes.

Hadn't they come with a machine to blow insulation

through walls?

Of course.

Just like everywhere else.

The insulation was—dirty.

That was a good enough word to use, and they couldn't deny a word like that. They all seemed to think that was the word to use. Arnold stood with his large coat, unusually large mittens and his large gumboots, and let the house melt from him. He sniffed now and then, an imperceptible little sniff. But he noticed. Seaweed noticed everything about himself, whom he had believed in just before Christmas for a moment. That really had been the best point in his life. Later he hated himself for ever thinking, "Craig is right."

"So the insulation has to come out," they said. "It's a matter of taking your walls down."

He sniffed again.

"Oh—it's a matter of taking my walls down," Mabel said, as if she shouldn't be surprised at this. In fact she wasn't surprised at all. It was simply a matter of tearing her walls down. She looked about the room, and seemed distracted.

"How much money do we get?" Harry said.

They couldn't tell him.

"Do each of us get a bunch—or does it come all in one lump sum?"

They couldn't tell him.

"Do we have to wait a long time, or will the cheques be here any day?" They couldn't tell him that either.

They couldn't tell them when the walls would be torn down either. Seaweed rubbed his tongue over his mouth in disgust.

He turned on the television in disgust. They looked at him in silence.

He drank a pop, and slurped it down, just to annoy them.

And on the television came the *Dukes of Hazzard*.

Craig came later in the day.

"You treat Randy like a slave," Arnold said.

"That's preposterous."

"Ahh."

"When does Randy go into the woods?" he said.

"Soon," Craig said.

"Ha."

"Soon—if I had more help from the community, some little involvement, we might have a grand cub pack."

They all began laughing. It was impossible, but for once they all laughed in unison. Craig said nothing more. He left quietly.

The road was in trouble.

What he was ashamed about was his own ignorance. Why had he allowed this to happen? There was no answer. Certainly they should try harder because everyone was tired of them. No-one paid much attention to Mabel's complaining at bingo, and Harry got not an ear, even from the old lady. When he told how his wife died and let you know every stark detail—he wasn't listened to. None of them were listened to. You could see in their eyes that it was best to leave them alone.

What became of the insulation business was nothing either. Certain that they were all to get money, they began planning ways to spend it. But no money came. Without hesitation, Harry and Sadie said they were going to sue the government. But nothing came of that either. For there was no insulation. They had put insulation in other houses and other people were suffering. But there was no insulation in their house. Mabel hadn't signed the form and they hadn't put it in. It came as no surprise to Arnold. They tested for insulation and found that there wasn't any. The government inspectors asked her if she ever remembered it being put in?

"Oh that's right—they didn't put it into our house—I never asked for it," Mabel said.

And the idea of money evaporated.

They became envious of other houses and other people.

And they took it out on one another. They squabbled over cookies and pop in the middle of the day. Everything would be going smoothly, and then someone would say something, and the rest would turn on him savagely.

"Where's our money?"

"Ha."

"Why didn't you ask for insulation?"

"I didn't because I knew it was bad."

"You knew it was bad—liar, you knew it was bad—whore."

"Don't call her a whore."

"Well—everyone will get a brand new house now—"

"No-one wants things like that in their house—it causes cancer."

"So—they'll get money. They'll get money."

"So what if it does cause cancer—that hasn't been proven—but everyone will get a new house," Harry said, holding up one finger.

"No-one will get a new house."

"Ahhh."

Every fortnight their cheques came. A cheque for Mabel—the biggest. A cheque for Arnold, the smallest. A cheque for Harry, which no-one saw, and a cheque for Sadie.

They planned their life not by the menu Juliet had written for them. They planned their meals at random, and ate what they could.

Juliet was disgusted.

So let her be.

So let the oil run out again.

"I tell you the fights are getting worse," Father Billy said. He hardly came anymore.

"So—find us a good social worker."

They glared at him.

"They promised us a new deal for the insulation."

"How can an alcoholic help us—people who don't drink."

Father Billy shrugged off an insult.

They glared at him.

All of them—even Harry—narrowed their eyes.

"They promised us," Sadie said, feebly. "They did—

they promised us."

Snow came into the back porch through the cracks in the porch's walls, and made little snakelike movements across the floor. Arnold hit Randy for no reason after school hour, as the bus chugged away in the dark, between glittering hopeful streetlights.

What crept into their life during this month was an awful envy, an envy that stole joy and happiness, an envy that bothered their very hair and made their eyes shift here and there. They were envious not because they had nothing, not because they were thin or fat, with black ankles and dirty underwear. Nor because Randy loved Craig, and Juliet was preparing to make changes in their very lives. What they were envious about was something else. Something very distasteful.

They were envious because their suffering seemed to count for nothing. That no-one knew it like they. That other people's suffering was spoken about. And they remained the same.

"Mr. Matheson's so sick that he'll lose his house now."

"Is he? What does he have to worry about, with his home and garden—his beautiful home and garden—he always had one."

"Yes—what has he suffered?"

"Yes—"

"There was a story about him in the paper, telling everyone how much he lost because of the insulation."

"They should tell a story about us."

"Yes—they should tell our story in the paper—how everyone's against us."

"Randy you get upstairs—"

"No."

"Get upstairs—"

One of them would be angered enough to hit him.

"Leave him alone."

"Leave me alone."

And so it would go on.

Oh yes, envy grated them, hit them like pile-drivers. He had returned to telling jokes in the most mediocre manner. Yet everyone laughed at them, so he felt that at least he was amusing someone.

Why do these people live this way, he would say.

Or why does such and such a country do this.

And he would tell the joke and make them laugh. It was very funny.

Sadie and he would eat jelly beans all afternoon, handing them back and forth in a sign of peace. She and he would sit up late at nights.

What they believed was this—that they needed a new social worker. They all believed it now. Besides, what did Juliet know about them?

"She went to college," Harry said.

"What do they teach you in college?"

"Physics," Mabel said, smiling suddenly.

"She can't even have a baby of her own," Harry said. "Imagine."

"She can't help us—we need a professional."

That word sprang from nowhere one cold February afternoon.

"She can't help us—she can't even have a baby."

"We need a professional."

And they all spoke at once.

"You liked her Mabel," Sadie said. "I'm sure you liked her more than anyone else—Seaweed and I were always on guard."

"Yes," Seaweed said, caught up with the moment.

"She'll pay."

"We'll get even."

Such was their conversation. It bled away to nothing.

He didn't know until that moment that Juliet couldn't have a child, but he pretended he'd always known it.

But envy was something that made him lie just as he had often heard others lie, tell stories, just as he heard others tell stories, and blaspheme just the same way.

They lived with themselves all night long. That is, they lived with each other's fear for their own health. Sadie cursed now and then about her eyes, which were red and sore. Mabel, dour, complained about her size, and her

107

legs swelling. Arnold complained about his spine, and how he was sure it was bending in two. Harry complained about his testicles and how they hurt. They lived with this commonality day in and day out.

They ruined each other's tempers and Arnold couldn't think. He scratched his head, and what do you think? It bled and brought bumps. Nor did he have a cat to blame it on—for fleas.

CHAPTER 19

One day, close to this time, when there was a red wind and nothing melted, and the blanket thrown over the back steps had frozen solid, Father Billy came to see them, for he had heard, or it was reported to him, that another fight had taken place—the television had been broken.

Actually the TV was broken. But no-one would take the blame for it. Everyone was too ashamed. For weren't they supposed to live like other people, with televisions?

There was a program on the night before, and a fight started because of it. Arnold caused terror by having a knife in his pocket, and walked up and down stairs with it, sticking out, blade first. Why he did this he was unsure of. When Harry sat down to watch his program, which was filled with gospel singing, Arnold decided to act.

"Ohhh," Harry said, "those songs make me inspired."

"Inspired—do they?" Arnold said. And he found out there and then, with a little discussion, that Harry had been sending money to those television programs— almost since he began watching them.

"How much money?" Mabel said. "How much?"

And with a further discussion, which wasn't too calm, Seaweed discovered that it wasn't his own money he was sending, but that he had gone into Mabel's purse—and into Seaweed's shoebox.

"It's for the best," he said. Arnold there and then kicked the television. It busted, and glass scattered and cut Randy's face, and Arnold's shoe caught on fire for some reason, and he had to run up and down stairs to put the shoe out. However, that's when he grabbed the knife and kept his vigil.

There was no use Mabel protesting. Mabel had pleaded with him not to start trouble—he knowing that she meant he shouldn't slice his belly again—for news of it would be all over the roadway in no time. Also, she had to hold Randy over the sink and let him bleed into it. People must have heard the shouts, for it was winter and sound carried over the naked ice in the blind wind. They all were ashamed of their fights. But they should have known that shame causes more fights than it prevents.

Throughout the night he caused terror in the house. It was one of his bad nights. A night to remember for sheer badness.

He wouldn't go to bed, and he stamped through the house with the knife in his pocket. The television had a big hole in it, shoesize, and smelled of burnt wires. Mabel had wanted to take it outside for fear of fire, but no, he wouldn't let her. They all went to their rooms, and he was left by himself to ponder his condition.

"Who wants a game of cribbage?" Or, "Come out and see me," were the constant words from his mouth.

He felt sorry for himself, it was true. And he talked himself out. He stared at Randy's blood that had splashed the sink, a few big drops on the counter near the breadbox. But one drop in particular was smaller and brighter than all the rest, and looked like Randy himself —all alone, away from everything, with his cub hat on.

But at this moment it only made him angry that he had caused anything to happen to his brother, and that he had acted so foul.

The wounded television was nothing; a picture of his soul.

Father Billy took him aside that morning and asked

him to reason. Be reasonable before you do more damage, before something inside you is seared off like a burnt vein. And so, not being certain whether he had any friends left in the house, they went into the shed and tried to find a spot in the bitter cold.

The priest's face was as red as the wind. Seaweed's hair looked limp and dusty, as if ready to fall out.

"It don't have scars though I've been in some good fights," Arnold said. He was nervous and his lips trembled.

"Yes."

"Except for one scar, which I gave myself."

The priest said nothing.

"I live near the river so I can smell the seasons as they come. It is a season where they have no use for me—so why should I care?"

Again the priest didn't answer.

"There's no use in fighting anymore—no use in complaining is there? All this past year I've been telling myself there's no use in complaining.

"But then—Harry sits at the supper table and talks about his wife—and how she died—and it's too cold to go anywhere, so I have to sit and listen to him—Sadie coaches him along, so not one detail is missed."

The priest shifted his weight and pulled his overcoat tighter.

Seaweed stopped long enough to light a cigarette. Here the priest moved forward a little bit to warm his hands over the flame from the Bic lighter.

"The prison keeps rearing its head in the cold behind me. The prison machinery keeps whining in the afternoon and the frozen lightbulb in the guard-shed busted one night last month. Then for two weeks of frozen waste there wasn't a sound.

"Sometimes I get irritated at Sadie it is true—even though I must remember she is an old lady, like you said —but she takes bubble baths all the time and doesn't clean our tub out. Now suppose one of us were to do that?

"The television crawled all over me day and night, and

it was time to do something about it.

"Mabel buys too many things from the Royal Family, and spends her money that way.

"It seems as if we are always getting tricked into believing who we are, or who we are supposed to be like. For the schoolgirls on this road, they are supposed to be like that girl on the billboard, wearing those jeans.

"It's no use to deny that I hated Harry right off the bat.

"Let me tell you that Mabel likes these stories about how his wife died, and her cheeks tremble all over.

"His hands are like white cookies."

After he had said this he believed he had said enough, and it was sufficient for the priest to understand him. The priest told him to forgive Harry for his hands, forgive Mabel for her interest in the Royal Family, forgive Sadie her bubble baths—and if it must come to that, then clean the tub out for her. Forgive the billboard also. Forgive and then your guilt and shame will disappear.

In fact he said the same things as he had said before. He coughed and pulled the coat around him. Arnold again had the feeling, as he had when he spoke to the student, Stephen, that he had said too much.

The most outlandish things they hoped for.

Without let up.

And soon there was another television set in place of the one that was kicked in.

The old one was thrown out into the snowdrift above the cot Arnold like to sit upon.

And the family watched television once more.

CHAPTER 20

March came in like a lion, all at once. Arnold was in a turmoil about it for he had sat here long enough. He wanted warm weather like others want blood in their veins. He sat on the stairs leading up to the dark rooms. Everyone knew why he sat there. Everyone knew what these rooms were like. They were little better than cupboards. So he said:

"We live here in the cold, in rooms like cupboards, so there."

He was trying to work himself into a state. It wasn't unusual for him in March, to begin at the first of the month and work himself into a state, so that by the end of the month he'd have something to be guilty over, something to feel bad about.

"How long have you been sitting there?" Sadie said.

"Never mind."

"If you've been sitting there longer than ten minutes you've been wasting time," she said.

"I don't waste time," he said, "I've nothing to do—so my time is my own—"

He grinned.

"I have to go upstairs," she said.

"Go ahead."

"Please move."

He took a peculiar notion and grinned.

"No."

She stepped back and looked at him. He saw that she was trying to control herself.

Light had fixed itself on the ironing-board in the kitchen, on the dark cloth that covered the hallway, on the iron that stood upright with its flat surface and the day itself was going backwards. Already the afternoon was lost. Already the evening was beginning.

"Ha," he said.

His skinny feet were pressed together. He had his socks on. And holes in his pant-legs; one at each knee-cap. He'd been here for a long time.

He'd sat here most of the afternoon, smoking cigarettes in the stale light. Light that was hampered by the dark little hallway. He decided that he no longer liked anyone. While he sat there certain reflections came to him. Randy was packing to go into the woods with the cubmaster. No-one offered Randy any advice on what to take into the woods, or how to dress for it. Mabel said she didn't know if she'd let him go, she thought it was a bad idea. Sadie said he should watch out.

"You should watch out," Sadie said. "That's all I have to say—"

"Watch out why can't you," Harry said.

Randy nodded, taking this as advice.

"Craig said we'll stay in a cabin," Randy said.

Seaweed wanted to say something bright and cheerful, but he couldn't.

"Why should he watch out," he said to Sadie. "You're always telling people to watch out."

"He should watch out—sure he should," Harry said.

Arnold sat on the stairs, taking this in. His eyes were black with unforgiveness. He couldn't bring himself to forgive anyone.

"Sadie kicked you when you were a baby—that's all I know," he said to Harry.

"I didn't," Sadie said, "that's all made up."

"Nothing is ever made up."

"It was—it was all made up—Momma never kicked me."

"How did you get bad testicles?"

And so it went on for a little bit. And then he shut up, until Sadie wanted to climb the stairs. It was obvious no-one would believe him when he said she was a bad influence. But that was so.

When she went to move around him he took a bad turn and wouldn't let her go up the stairs.

"I'll tell your mother," she said.

"Go ahead."

Her legs pressed against his. The stairs were dark like a sad crawlway, filled with smoke that no-one noticed. In the back porch the garbage was beginning to stink again, a cold fly sat upon the plastic garbage bag and kicked itself in the head. So everything was just starting.

"I wouldn't go up there if I were you—we've been

113

invaded."

"What do you mean—'we've been invaded?'" she said.

He looked at her.

"Rats."

"There are no rats here," she said.

"How do you know?"

"They've all been frozen off—when they moved the dump across the river and ploughed the old site over, all the rats were frozen. I saw their feet sticking up."

"That was last winter."

"Yes."

"Well now there are new ones."

He was having a good time of it, and had forgotten the pains in his head. Pain that had stabbed him just like scissors for two days.

Then he said he was going out to kill Jerry.

So the night didn't go well. A fresh storm had started, and snow swept about him, and gathered in the fields. It was a warm storm. He didn't button his coat until he wanted to light a cigarette.

Jerry in fact had been waiting for him on the road, as if their souls had communicated.

Arnold watched him walk to meet him.

Jerry sang:

"Bad news travels like wildfire
Good news travels slow
People call me ole wildfire
Everywhere I go
Cause I'm bad news."

He had a good voice—very much his own, and Arnold nodded, appreciatively.

When Arnold blinked Jerry punched him in the head, and a thumb grazed his eye. He fell down and curled up and then was kicked. People said he was kicked unconscious but he never thought he was—but once, when he was hit on the back of the head, his teeth came out in two pieces, and rattled across the ice like a plastic skeleton's.

All he could say was:

"Beat me some more why don't you—okay then beat me some more—"

He thought he said that at least twenty times, but people said he said it only twice. However it went, he lost his earmuffs in the snowbank, and couldn't find them the next day.

He thought Jerry got tired of kicking him after a while, but people said Trenda came running down the road and hauled Jerry away.

So he sat on the stairs thinking of this.

He thought of all the crises in his house, one crisis after another. And most of them were his fault. If he wanted to own up.

Mabel screamed and roared, when she saw him. That was worse than anything else. Randy cried. Randy still had the patch on his face where he'd been cut by flying glass, and Arnold's small nose was broken now, and his teeth, which someone had retrieved for him from across the road, were carried about in his pocket.

Sadie said:

"Well you got yours—"

She said that twice, but Arnold looked at her just like he had the night he'd torn her Harlequin romances, and she said nothing else. Except to herself. To herself (which was overheard by everyone) she said she knew a lot of fighters that were better than others, and always went out with the best fighters when she was a girl. The best fighters were her choice above anyone else.

Arnold brooded on the stairs. If only he'd been more determined, things might have been different.

Snowfall never made it seem like Christmas again. Yet snow fell night after night. But perhaps it was a good sign—for ever since he had taken to looking for signs from things, he had noticed them everywhere—the red wind in the sky meant February torment, and brushed his nerves with fire—the melting ice on the eaves of houses meant the robins would come sooner, and he'd be lucky in playing the video games for money—a wood-

115

pecker meant a thief, and he would soon see one—a crow meant death if it came near to his house.

Soot from chimneys blowing away with sparks meant someone visiting from far away—though no-one came.

A meteor falling from the sky meant a loss at hockey—a loss to his beloved Canadiens.

If he wore his socks inside out it meant he would lie before the day was out.

Spitting through his stream of urine meant he would have good luck and money tomorrow.

These things he took as fact and truth though there was no evidence of them.

The snow fell downward. The trees and the air were silent as a moon, black and comforting.

Ahhh.

The road was silent. All was driven with snow and the trees stood frozen like upturned straw in a stall. Some of the elms had had their tops cut off—and some had had their bottoms cut too and remained stumps. All were now signs from heaven, but it was unfortunate how badly he read them.

He did not have good luck playing the video games—and lost $13.

People couldn't help grinning when they saw him, because his nose was broken and one eye was swollen shut, and he carried his teeth about in his pocket.

He had to hide from the RCMP who'd come to see them. He hid in the bedroom closet. At his feet lay Randy's old lunchbucket with Pluto and Goofy.

"There's been no fights here," Sadie said.

"No fights," Mabel said.

"No-one fights about this place—we have a nice road," Harry said.

So the RCMP left.

Everyone laughed. They laughed when he came out of the closet with his nose broken.

Later he and Harry tried to glue his teeth but it didn't work.

No crow appeared near his house—but a moosebird

looking for bread.

The day before Randy left for the woods Mabel had a change of heart. Seaweed had always seen her like this, and took it in stride. She hired a taxi and went into town. She bought Randy new boots and a knapsack, with "Cub-Scouts of Canada" on it. It had a red maple leaf. She bought him woollen socks and heavy gloves. She bought him all kinds of candy, so he'd be able to treat everyone. He thanked her and she kissed him, smothering him in kisses. She kissed his eyes and face, rubbed his bones and sat him on her knee.

Seaweed looked out the window.

"What are you looking for?" Randy said.

Seaweed said nothing.

"You're not looking for someone to get even with?" Randy asked.

"No."

"We'll all get even somehow."

Arnold said nothing.

Randy went to the window. His nose ran and his mouth was stained by hard toffee. He still had the bandage, smelling of yellow antiseptic, on his cheek, where he'd been cut with flying glass. In fairness he had forgiven everyone, yet Seaweed felt apprehensive. That was how the innocent got even—by showing their wounds.

Envy still grated them all at times, about the ureaformaldehyde—but no-one, except Sadie, showed it anymore. She was sure they had been cheated out of a grand chance. But no longer did Arnold wish to discuss it. She couldn't get a rise out of him about it, so he felt he had accomplished something.

Sometimes they'd meet in the kitchen and begin to talk about it.

"Your mother's a stupid fat toad."

He'd look at her and blink twice.

"And you are a toadling," she would spit.

He'd blink some more. Blink.

"Ureaformaldehyde," he would answer.

"Don't say that to my mother," Harry would caution,

"she's an old woman."

Father Billy—whom Arnold had taken to calling Private Billy for some reason, told him that this was because of living at close quarters.

So he minded his own business. That was always on his lips after the beating he had taken:

"I'm just a man who minds his own business."

The road told him everything.

Some said the next thing they would build in the province was a second nuclear power plant.

But what was nuclear power to Seaweed?

It was nothing.

One night he had an argument with Harry about the Russians, and said he hoped there would be another war fairly soon—though he admitted that Canada had only one ship.

Harry told him he would burn in hell if a war came now, because he swore around the house, and didn't help with things. Then Harry said he'd been in two or three wars that Seaweed knew nothing about.

But what was that to him?

Seaweed then made up a story about his father, and said that he was killed in Vietnam, though this wasn't true. And he had lied badly.

Then Harry said that Randy must then be a bastard.

So that's how the argument ended, always at the point of no return. With Sadie keeping score.

The road told him the truth.

The roadway—this endless stretch of road, dark and broken as anywhere in Canada, told him everything.

He never forgave Harry his hands like white cookies.

He never forgave Randy who'd begun to pee the bed again because of some nervousness in his character.

He never forgave Mabel her two colour pictures, of the Prince and Princess, tacked up beside the Queen.

"But what does a Princess care," Sadie said.

He left the Christmas tree where it was, because of perversity.

He was gone for a week. Some people said he was out drunk, and others agreed.

When he came home he slipped into the house quietly so as not to wake anyone, but Sadie was up anyway.

She told him he was an uncaring son and brother, and had no manners.

"So—what's that to you?—people should mind their own business."

Harry said that that was the answer he expected. Then he told how his wife died of shingles. He told the whole story from beginning to end—all the itching baths and everything. Then he shook his head.

Then they told him that Randy had had a bad accident in the woods—either a tree had fallen on him, or he had fallen out of a tree, but they weren't sure which, and that Mabel had gone in for an emergency operation. Both of them were in bad shape.

They saw him shaking, and unable to control himself anymore. It brought all kinds of spots before his eyes.

"So there," Harry said. "That was something you didn't know."

He went to the hospital every day to visit Mabel who had had an operation, and Randy who was in a coma, because a tree had fallen on him or he had fallen out of a tree, he didn't know which.

Seaweed refused to take a taxi, and he walked down the road alone, trying to flag cars down. Harry hired taxis because they were paid for by the social services. Sadie went with him now and again.

But Arnold, drawing on his courage, refused to do this. It was cold, and the warming of March had not come yet. It was uncomfortable to breathe more than twice in twenty seconds. The road, raw and bright, as if winter had refused to go away, though he prayed for its end, bled into the horizon and all the houses came closer to his eye.

It was a dark misunderstood part of his life. In fact he didn't understand anything. And sometimes he could be

seen with a look of wild self-pity on his face, and sometimes his face was very hard.

He was sure everything was going to be all right
though. And when he got up in the morning he said to
himself:

"They'll be better today."

And he'd begin the cold walk. Once in the hospital,
after his ears had thawed out (for he had lost his earmuffs in the fight) and the heat began to change the
colour of his flesh, he sat in the waiting-room. He sometimes sat there for hours at a time. Every time a doctor
went by, Seaweed would anticipate a consultation.

The doctor (the same one his mother went to see) did
consult with him, and explained everything to him—his
mother had had an operation.

Randy was in a coma, but they could only hope for the
best.

After this consultation Seaweed felt that he knew more
than he did before. He bought himself a pop, and talked
to everyone in the waiting-room.

"My brother's in a coma, and my mother has had an
operation."

His teeth chattered and he nodded to himself. People
nodded also.

Some people were kind enough to ask questions:

Where do you come from?

What do you do?

What do think of this or that?

Seaweed asked if Randy had fallen out of a tree, or had
a tree fallen on him, but no-one seemed to know.

"The cub-master's very upset—"

"I see," Arnold said politely.

The next day, the doctor saw him, smiled and was too
busy to say more than hello.

He saw Mabel that afternoon.

She told him that she had had an operation and smiled
at him so weakly it brought butterflies.

"Yes," he said, "I know."

She went to take his hand—but this confused him, and

he backed away, hitting his snowboots together. They were made of rubber. She told him that they had given her a bath before they examined her, but Arnold told her they did that with everyone and it didn't mean that she was dirty.

But this bothered her, and he couldn't reconcile her to it.

He couldn't get it out of her mind, though he yawned to show it didn't bother him.

The doctor was no more than a decade older than Seaweed. And Seaweed felt fierce and haughty in his wild clothes, and his eyes fluctuated between kindness and malevolence. The doctor told him he had taken over both cases, that the cubmaster had come in to see Randy, and was very upset.

"Nothing like this has happened to him before."

Arnold lowered his eyes, looked at the floor and at a white flat gurney stretched out like a body. Then he became ashamed.

The doctor had a sharp nose and sandy hair. He had large eyes that were always saying more than he actually said. When he walked, his coat trailed behind him, and he carried things in his pockets.

No-one told Arnold anything, so he became stubborn. He sat in the waiting-room and refused to move. He wouldn't lift his feet when the janitor came in to sweep the floor.

"Could you lift your feet buddy?"

"Go to hell."

This attitude got him nowhere. People were fed up with him very soon.

When he went home, he couldn't stand the talk.

"People in comas usually don't come out of them—"

"No—"

"Why doesn't Mabel come home?"

He cleaned out the tub one night and had a bath, scrubbing his lathered head for an hour.

He didn't go back to the hospital the next day because it was Sunday and he didn't know he was allowed to. He had the old idea that everything stopped on Sundays.

The whole road saw what he was doing, and how stupidly he walked amidst the glare of sun and raving squalls of snow. While others took taxis he walked, and that was something to consider. Everyone called it determination, even Father Billy.

But the end was to come also.

He got angry and the idea of getting even plagued his days. Scorn washed over him. In fact, he wasn't very friendly with anyone.

Not Juliet who brought him up a chicken dinner.

"Did Randy fall out of a tree or did a tree fall on him?"

"I don't know," she whispered. She had washed, fluffy hair, like the tail of a cat. Not a cat he would have, but a cat someone else would have—someone who could take care of kittens.

"Well what we don't know can't hurt us," he said.

Not the minister who told him about God's plan. When the minister spoke Arnold kept looking at the little heap the janitor had swept into the corner. Arnold had settled down to eat his chicken dinner when the minister arrived one day. He had his knees pressed together and the plate upon his knees, and he was shaking pepper onto his mashed potatoes. He did this with increasing fury, until the potatoes were black.

"Well," the minister said, "I see you've gotten something to eat."

"Don't think you're going to get any," Arnold said.

Visiting Mabel shortly became a bother to Harry, who called Mabel his wife, and to Sadie. That left only himself. But not before having an argument with him in the waiting-room.

Sadie stopped coming.

"It's high time Mabel came home," she said. "And started behaving herself."

"Leave her alone," Arnold said.

"Don't think I'll be back here—not if you begged me."

"Who makes your meals?" Arnold said.

"Ha."

Arnold said:

"I should kill you—maybe I will, think about it."

"You're just ungrateful," Harry said.

They all started fighting. One would say something and the other would respond—hoping he'd said the last word. But getting the last word in wasn't easy. Everyone could hear them and it became a terrible scene, with Sadie fixing her hair.

His nerves were bad. He sat beside Randy all night talking to him about bingo. Why he chose bingo as a subject he didn't know. They had placed Randy on a machine to keep his heart going.

"In cases like this—it's best not to bother him too much."

The doctor told him.

And Arnold felt relieved. But then he didn't know what the case was about.

He brought Bruce's picture in:

"Love ya Mabel," it read.

"Who is that?" the nurse asked him.

"No-one."

The nurse looked at the picture—the frame had broken the night he'd kicked the television, but otherwise it was all right.

"Why don't you go home," the nurse said. "You can't do anything here."

But he waited. He looked like he'd been kicked again. And he often said:

"It's just a rotten kick in the head."

One night he remembered something—another year had passed:

"This spring I'm going to kill seals," he said.

"How could you kill one of those little creatures?" the nurse asked. She smiled at him and he loved her.

"With a club."

He began to hate the hospital. Babies were being born, and he couldn't stand to see that they were, and people laughed and talked about all sorts of things: weather, politics, hockey. But when they asked him his opinion he had none.

For why have opinions? They only got you into trouble.

The only one he became close to was Juliet. For some reason he became close to her for three days in a row.

Then there were fights between him and the nurses.

"You can't sing in here."

"Why—it's just to pass the time."

"Do you want to be put out of the hospital?"

"Go to hell—"

"You'll disturb the patients."

"You're disturbing my patience."

Thinking this was a great retort he said it to everyone.

"I'll disturb the patients—well, they're disturbing mine," he said.

After this Juliet was sharp with him, and there was only one nurse he trusted.

The nurse took him aside. And he fell in love for the first time since last year. It seemed that only this nurse, with her coal-black hair and blue eyes, loved him enough to take care of Randy and his mother. She asked about his eye, and how it got yellow, and he told her he was punched. She smoothed his mop-red hair with her hand, and touched his elbow, quite bony by most standards.

She told him his mother was on oxygen and he could wait for the doctor to tell him what had happened.

He sat in the waiting-room, but the doctor didn't come by.

"Well she's on oxygen now, but she'll be all right tomorrow."

Then, for a time, he refused to go back to the hospital. His idea was that the hospital brought out the worst in him. He was either angry or sad. And who could he shout at? To shout at these people would never solve anything—and he'd come from a home where to shout was ordinary and necessary.

Juliet wondered where he was.

Why didn't he go to the hospital?

Why didn't he take an interest—didn't he want to see

the doctor, or learn what was happening?

"I guess you just don't care for your mother," Sadie said.

"No he don't," Harry said.

"Why don't you go to the hospital today—?"

"Why don't you—?"

"It's my arthritis dear—it's my old bones—I'm just dying in bits and pieces."

"Don't call me dear!"

"As you wish."

"I won't take dear from you—"

"Then go to the hospital—"

"No!"

What was wrong with a boy who wouldn't go to the hospital, and left loved ones alone?

The road began to ask this question. It asked it again and again, and he became perverse. He brooded. He sat on the stairs with his teeth in his pocket.

Sadie told stories. She began to tell them one night and continued to.

"Poor little Randy," she would begin.

"Remember when he gave me the flowers—I cry my old eyes out thinking of it." Or, "He saved a peanut-butter sandwich all day long, just for Arnold."

"Don't think Craig doesn't know what goes on in this house—Craig knows all about it—"

This is how they continued. He knew they were trying to drive him out of the house—into the night that was swept like a desert.

He stared into the wall. It was always the wall, with homes made from black boots. It was only the wall, the wall forever, and he would always stare at one or another, and it would be silent.

Somehow blame is only given to those who are willing to accept it, to those whose scorn turns inward, whose hatred diminishes themselves.

"We aren't like anyone else," he'd say.

But then he'd say:

"Perhaps we are like other people—we just show it

more."

He didn't go back to the hospital for many days.

Craig came to see him.

He was sitting in his room. His expression was one of lead on a cold evening, lead as white as twilight, as flickering lights on October afternoons.

Craig was a big man with a large mouth, a full moustache. He sat on the edge of the bed, as if he were invited to sit there, and as if this were normal.

Craig spoke of the accident.

"It's a terrible thing to lose a boy," he said. "In the woods—it never happened before—one minute we were all together, I was making a list of duties—you see we have always made a list of duties to go along with the trip; duties give children a sense of security."

Arnold nodded.

"Duties are imperative to the whole affair."

Arnold nodded.

Not once did Arnold look him in the face.

"Do you know—I thought Randy was special—he was very special to me—"

Arnold nodded, looking at his socks.

Craig smiled.

He explained that he didn't send Randy outside alone —they used a different system.

There were a few things bothering Arnold.

"Was there enough room in the cabin for everyone?"

"Of course," Craig answered.

Arnold looked relieved—as if this were the main point.

"Yes—I knew there was," he said.

This was the point he seemed to question more than any other, and once Craig answered it, all seemed right with the world once more.

"Did he fall out of a tree, or did a tree fall on him?" Arnold asked.

Craig said that he wasn't sent to the river in the dark to fetch water, and that this is what he heard people were saying, and this is what he wanted to clear up.

Arnold couldn't answer.

Craig then said that he didn't feel children had enough rights in our present society, and that's why so many of them turned into bad apples.

This was true.

So Arnold nodded, and Craig shook his head.

He began to tremble. He kept brushing his fingers through his hair, hair like a wire brush, and Craig said nothing.

Craig kept shaking his head. Arnold felt then that he could trust Craig more than any other man. He was worried, he said, because he'd heard Craig made Randy go outside—on purpose—as a punishment, and Randy's ears froze—but that must be untrue. Suddenly he looked up, as if he'd been stuck with a pin.

"I'll tell you—it's the doctor's fault," Arnold said bitterly, his eyes wild. "It's all his fault and no-one else's."

It took him a whole night to realize what he'd said, and who he'd blamed. Craig had gone home, and he sat alone. All along he'd thought that if he could carry a knife in his pocket, he would get even with Craig, but instead he hadn't even blamed him. He blamed the doctor with the big eyes. And he didn't know why. He had no idea why he said or did things this way, but everything he said and did seemed to be coming to a head.

The reason he didn't go to the hospital weighed upon him also. He was ashamed of everything. He was ashamed that his mother wasn't getting better, and he was ashamed that the doctor didn't want to speak to him very often. He was ashamed that he'd talked about bingo all night long to Randy—who mustn't have heard him anyway. He was ashamed he sang songs. He was ashamed he'd eaten a chicken dinner in front of the minister.

He was ashamed that he'd gone to the hospital in the last while hoping to see the nurse, with her white skirt.

These are the things he thought of. It wasn't right to go to a hospital to look at the nurses.

"Everything will be better tomorrow," he said.

Yet he knew nothing would be better. Unless he himself made an end.

127

The next day he knew why Sadie wanted him out of the house. She wanted him gone because Cy Ramsey was coming to see her, and bringing a bottle.

They sang songs together, and Sadie stumbled from one wall to another when she drank.

Cy told her that he had Norman working for him.

They laughed at this, as if it were a joke.

"I will kill somebody," Arnold said.

He stood in his dirty underwear and complained of being kept awake.

"It's after one o'clock, you should be up—" Sadie said.

"I haven't slept all night long," he said politely, "so I must sleep now—so you see Cy—since I haven't slept all night long—Craig came here with information—you see —so I have to sleep now—so maybe you could come back some other day."

"Who in hell are you?" Cy said.

"Yes," Harry said, "who in hell are you?"

"I'm Arnold," he said politely, "and I think I'll remain Arnold."

"Arnold's got a dirty arse," Cy said.

Arnold knew he wanted their sympathy, because his mother was in the hospital and Randy was in a coma.

And this bothered him more than anything else.

The Christmas tree still stands in the room, like our very own butler.

Father Billy came here to slap me in the face, but that's his right.

"What happened to you?" he said. "Why don't you visit your dying flesh and blood—I've just come from them."

I said nothing. It was after Cy had left. The room, the tragic living-room that no-one entered or left, felt sad, as if Cy had brought sadness into the room and Sadie had joined in with it, and I, stinking as I was, at least wanted nothing but sleep, until they started tormenting me— and then I wanted their sympathy.

"Get the hell out of here," Sadie said to the priest.

She took my side for once.

It was a good feeling.

"Ya," Harry said. "Leave him alone."

So Father Billy stopped slapping me and left the house, and I sat alone in the room, still undressed, and let the cold crawl over me. But March is going; I can smell it.

Then they started in again.

"Mabel," Harry said. He started to compare her to his first wife, and tried to make the comparison interesting, but I didn't listen. He said both of them were fat, poor.

"Both of them were fat and poor," he said.

He blamed Sadie for kicking him in the testicles when he was a child.

Sadie didn't listen.

She wondered if they were going to die.

And then she said she knew they were.

She knotted her hands about the couch covers until I could hear scratches.

The hornets came alive at an odd hour, as if it were twice as warm as it should be.

Sadie made frantic scratches, as if death had already invaded the house properly, and the coffins had already entered.

Sadie then said it was all Craig's fault—and she smoothed her hair, it hadn't been dyed in a long while and it was streaked with grey. Grey lingered in the room.

"Only I know how long the nights are here," Sadie said.

Her body was a sad wisp, as impartial to life as most things I've seen.

I tried to reassure them that no-one would die—death didn't come overnight I said. I sat with my chest bare, and my chest rattled when I breathed, not from illness, but from pure disagreement.

Death doesn't come overnight I said.

Sadie said she was afraid it did.

Harry said that he was kicked in the testicles as a child and managed only to have fat women who didn't care for sex.

It was too close to me to talk about. I remembered the day Randy came home from the foster home, when there were birds in the warm birdnests, waiting to fly, and the prison they were building scraped away in the heat. What I had thought of that day I couldn't for anything remember. Something about Trenda. Was that the week my mother's purse was stolen—or was it further back than that?

No-one remembered.

Sadie told me that Mabel wearing her old heavy grey coat always sat alone at bingo—at the third table, on a wooden bench and played eight cards, and kept the markers in her purse to pretend she had more money than she did.

"I don't think she ever had any friends," Sadie said.

Harry said she had a lot of friends, and that he knew them all—they were his friends also.

"No."

"Yes she did."

"No she didn't at all."

"Yes of course she did."

And so it went on. It was just like sitting with them in the waiting-room.

"I always had brains," Harry said, rubbing his nose.

Ahhh.

I waited. I saw red in the television set. I saw the breeze in the room. The way the wind blew.

"Death doesn't come overnight," I said.

"Yes it does," Harry sniffed. "It comes like a thief—"

"But not two at once," I cautioned.

"That's God's choice," Sadie said.

"God's wisdom," Harry said.

Sadie scratched her long fingers upon the yellow couch, and our room slowly filled with smoke. Now and then there was a car on the highway, passing us with a delinquent sound. I don't know why.

"Look," Sadie said. "the doctor made a mistake—he shouldn't have operated on Mabel."

"No—he shouldn't have operated—" Harry said.

"Of course he shouldn't have," Sadie said.

"What do we know now that we didn't know before?"

"Let's take her to another hospital."

"Yes—put them both in another hospital—"

But none of us knew what other hospital to take them to. We looked at each other, as if waiting for an answer. For the first time I saw that Harry was trying to take charge.

"Shut up," I said.

Sadie told him to shut up.

He stopped speaking. None of us knew what to do. We didn't know any other hospital.

"If the doctor made a mistake he'd tell us," Sadie said.

We were silent.

"Then why is she on a breathing-machine—and tubes stuck in her arms—?"

"I don't know—she had an operation—"

"But she was supposed to be home in a week."

"So the doctor made some mistake—"

We were silent.

"Let's take her to another hospital," Harry said.

He nodded to us, sitting in his undershirt. I said nothing. His skin was haggard and white, filled with abnormal sacks and pouches. But he nodded again, showing the bald spot on the top of his head.

"Cubs aren't so bad," Sadie said. "We shouldn't blame the cubs."

The nurse saw him running through the hospital. She took his hand.

His mouth looked like mash. His teeth had gone and the cut under his lip had re-opened. Why did he try to cry? He hadn't been expected to. If anyone were expected to cry it would have been someone else.

Norman and his new girlfriend were with him.

He sniffed, and searched about his pockets. The nurse took his hand.

"Look," he said.

But he had nothing to show them, and it was just a remark. Other than this he attempted to be quiet. Then he looked savagely at all the outpatients, and tried to frighten them. Most of them looked away from him. A few didn't—and even in his most horrible state didn't humour him.

He had Randy's cub-hat in his pocket.

It was an injustice to give it to him. But that's what Craig wanted to do.

"Poor little fellow," Norman's girlfriend said, because she didn't know what else to say. Then she shut up.

Arnold went back to the waiting-room. He had just bought himself a ham sandwich, and had one bite of it. He gave it to the nurse.

The nurse took his hand.

Craig said:

"Tell me who you want, and we'll make the arrangements."

"Therefore," Arnold said politely.

When he left the hospital, Arnold made sure he collected all their things, in two bags. Everyone looked at him. He walked into the bright sunshine, and smelled car tires, and carried the parcels under his arms. Norman and his girlfriend followed him toward the taxi.

"Therefore," Arnold said politely.

He forgot it was Easter Sunday.

A man passed them on the street with his boots unzippered. There were puddles now, where the snow had melted, and black pavement. So everything was just beginning. Sparrows, pigeons and blackbirds could be seen in the blue sky. The earth smelled fresh and lovely as if it were turning warmer by the minute.

CHAPTER 21

Smoke in the white sky, and the ice moved slowly away. The prison had a Canadian flag, and he was surprised it did.

Who knows what Norman will do? he thought one afternoon.

That was his first thought in many days.

He felt sad when he looked about the yard. Brown grass lay silent and the wind crawled up his legs.

"I should have a pint of rum," he thought.

And he walked into town and got two.

He came back home and drank one on the porch, and when he was drunk he went out into the back stubble and began to dig a garden. He fell down.

He crawled around outside until dark, because no-one cared where he was. The grass was long and he crawled through it with only his crinkly red hair showing. Everyone wondered where he was going to.

He tried to sing:

"Like a fox—like a fox on the run."

And he was conscious most of the time.

"Jerry is probably the only friend I have," he said to himself.

Some time after that, when the first warm days came, he went back to the Arcade.

There was no-one there. The doors were locked, the windows boarded and through the chinks of pane he could see that all the games had been removed. Donkey Kong was gone, and so was Outrider. Only an outlet or two was visible in the beam of white light. Other than that it looked just like a barn, as it always was.

He lit a cigarette and sat down on the plywood steps, watching a family of ants beneath his boots. He didn't dare kill one for bad luck. When one of the boys went by he said:

"Where is everything?"

"Mr. Johnson moved away," the boy told him. "When he lost his house because of the ureaformaldehyde he decided to move—and there was no-one to take over for him."

He offered the boy a cigarette, for the company—just to have someone to talk to—but the boy was anxious to get to where three girls were sitting, on a ledge a little farther away.

"I'm sorry to hear about your trouble," the boy said.

"My whole family died simultaneously," Arnold said. He snapped his fingers and shook his head.

It wasn't comfortable in the house anymore. Anyone could walk in and take what they wanted as far as he was concerned.

He didn't want to visit the graves. They looked like peanut shells cast upon the dirt.

Father Billy told him he must take stock of himself.

"Yes," he said.

To jar him out of depression the priest told him he was sorry for anything he said the night he slapped him in the face.

"That's all right," Arnold said.

Day followed day after this. False spring, when everything seemed to make a truce, and in any direction you looked you saw warm skies and hazy smoke from burning grasses, and then snow flurries again, and bitter days when cinders went flying in the dark.

A truce was recognized in the house. Sadie showed she could do for herself quite well. She no longer took her meals from the community, but bought herself a steak now and then and fried potatoes and boiled cabbage. She and Harry approached him one night:

"I suppose you'll be wanting us to leave," Sadie said.

"Why should I?" he said.

After this, whenever they wanted to do anything, they came to ask his approval.

"Can Sadie take Mabel's room?" Harry said one evening.

"Of course—why not."

Another night, Sadie said:

"Arnold do you think Mabel would have minded if I took those slippers?"

"Take them—why not?"

Sadie especially seemed to like him now. Some evenings she read Randy's letter from the foster home. He never knew why she did that, because it always made him cry.

He apologized to them one night.

"I'm sorry I never grew."

"What does that matter," Harry said. Harry, too, tried to be compassionate. There were only three left.

"I don't know—but I'm sorry I never grew—if I had grown I would have worked in the woods, and taken care of everyone."

He went and got another tattoo.

"What do you want on it?" the woman asked him.

"Just put Seaweed," he said.

So Seaweed was written in blood across his shoulder. But she was a nice old lady with tattoos of her own.

She had tattooed Norman.

And Jerry.

Often he didn't go home. He couldn't be found anywhere.

He'd be seen the next afternoon staggering home, his pants soaking wet and covered with burdocks.

It still smelled of winter in the lilac bushes yet summer in the splitting buds. Birds sounded shrill. He drank many evenings, and sang commercial jingles in the back shed.

He forgot.

What did he forget?

"What was my brother's name?" he asked.

"Randy of course."

"Oh—yes."

This morbidity wasn't any good. The priest was informed.

Cy Ramsey began bringing a bottle into the house and he and Sadie would drink it. One night he told Arnold he should get a new couch.

He paid Cy $20 for the couch, in advance, and Cy thanked him.

Then he forgot completely about it, so when the couch didn't come, it didn't bother him.

"These things in Mabel's room must bring you bad memories," Cy said to him.

"I've never thought about it."

"If her dresser and bed were sold, I could move my things into her room," Sadie said.

It seemed like the right thing to do.

"Well I'll have to sell them for you," Cy said. Every day Cy would come, and once in a while he had things figured out.

"Look," he said, "there's no need of Randy's bicycle here. It causes everyone pain—I'll have to sell it."

It was another good idea.

Sadie would put a rinse in her hair, which made her look like someone he'd seen in a history book—and dress up in huge earrings.

Cy told her she was a good woman—who'd held her own in a life of trouble.

The next afternoon she said:

"I'm a good woman—who's held my own in a life of trouble."

The house was murky, the hornets, after their catnap, came out of various holes.

And when it got darker, that is when the lights on the road fed the twilight, Cy and she staggered about, singing.

But this man was nothing to Seaweed.

So what did it matter?

"Aren't you going to visit the graves?"

"No—I refuse to."

No-one recognized him after that. He had his head shaved. He believed it would make him look manly, but he didn't realize how black his skull would look—like someone had shaken pepper over his head. His face was as white as a soda cracker, and the bit of hair he'd left upon himself ran across the top of his head like a strip of flypaper.

She stumbles about the house—this place. She walks on her little feet, and unsteadily brushes the wall.

"You're no man," she says to me. "Who are you trying to be? Shaving the only hair God gave you. Who are you?"

"Arnold."

This whole head-shaving business is a bad trick. My blemishes show much more. For instance I have pimples I never knew I had.

So.

So they have left and gone away.

Juliet and Craig.

In the evening I leave the house. They are working on the road below me—they are working on the prison. They are working everywhere it seems.

I go to the police station.

"You want to arrest someone—have an inquest—on someone. Forget the Norwegian—he's old news. Arrest Juliet and Craig."

I don't realize how loud I am talking.

He looks at me mildly, and then tells me to leave before they lock me up for my own good.

"I have friends on this road—I have Billy the priest," I tell him. My voice is calm.

For the first time in a month, I'm determined to get even.

I've gone to the doctor's office to demand pills. I sit in his office and look at the wall, with a healthy child staring at me.

"He doesn't have any hair," the child whispers to his father. They both stare at me, then the father tells him not to be rude. The child giggles out loud and wiggles its legs.

You think Norman cares for me. Not when he's mixed up with a girl who's telling him what to read.

He plans to go to university. It is all bad.

"There will be no prison here," he says.

"But they are building it every day."

"And so what," he says. "Listen, why don't you live with me?"

"Why? I can take care of myself."

Yet Norman never once had to shave his head. He

hides his tattoos.

Seaweed etched in blood across my shoulder is somewhat infected.

Norman works all day in the woods, and at night he goes to school. There is a scent of goodness about him, like sunlight upon a white tablecloth.

It was a difficult thing to do, to sign the house over to Cy and Sadie, but they were the only two willing to pay the back taxes. I can see no hope living in this house. They are ploughing the road away, and our house teeters upon the edge.

Old memories are like cranberries in the sun, like pebbles on a tin roof, like ice in a ditch. Old memories are like a balm to ease pain, are like a nail driven in your spine, are like a shadow across the sky with heavy wings. Are like a full gourd in a well near grass so green its odour stains you, near fish-and-chip stands on lonely highways, straight as a bolt.

Weather-beaten men when they pull nets.

Girls who laugh because they love.

Are chinks of pavement broken up in the back of a lonely province.

Memories are life's casualties long before the end is near.

To make you suffer in houses with boot marks and stabbed walls.

So I sit here many nights. I'm not alone. Outside the once-a-year circus has set up, on grounds that face the water. A dog or two barks at the transients, with their bold lively faces.

I am reading the transcript the nurse kept of my mother's last visit to the hospital. It is only now I realize things about it. The nurse has brought it to me after hesitating, and tells me things I know will bother my nerves. For if I thought I was helpless in the hospital before, now I know it to be true.

The nurse is frightened of me—I see that. I look like a creature in the darkness that hasn't been fed. This is what I've always wanted, in the back end of this province, to be able to frighten them—the bastards who have taken everything away (or so I think)—yet I manage only to frighten this poor woman who's frightened already—of the transcript that sits across her knee.

"Here," she tells me, "when the pain started—ninth of March."

"What's this?" I say.

"An IV."

"For what?"

"Anticoagulant."

"Yes." I don't understand, so I shouldn't pretend I do. I haven't understood anything in a while.

"To thin someone's blood," she says.

I let out a long sigh, like a bubble in a tube.

"The doctor guessed her to have a blood clot."

"Ahh."

"So her blood was thinned in the hopes of clearing it."

"Ahh."

"And this helped kill her—there wasn't any blood clot."

I don't answer. For what is there to say?

"She had a large infection after the operation—"

"Why?"

"Because he had cut her bowel open."

"An accident?"

"Of course."

"I see."

She sits beside me close enough to whisper in her ear, and even to reach out and stick my finger in it if I wanted to. Her ear in the almost darkness. Her ear in the room I'm ashamed to show her.

"When did he know?"

"He operated again—see, St. Patrick's day."

"Then he knew?"

"Sometimes people are headstrong—they don't want to believe they've made a mistake."

I said nothing.

"Shouldn't someone know?" she asked.

"That's up to you—"

"Aren't you interested?"

I shrugged again.

"It doesn't matter?"

"Of course not."

The nurse was thinking. Her eyes screwed up. She was probably thinking the same thing I was.

She left me, very lightly on her feet. Much like Craig had so many hours before, but I forget now how many hours have passed.

I wanted to tell the nurse I loved her. I wanted to hold her. She looked frightened. A hardened criminal is one who feels pain, and all types of burning indignities, but feels nothing for others.

So Billy the priest told me—a year and a half ago.

Seaweed knew something about the impertinence of power without questioning it or even knowing that he did. When he was bullied on the street, he said:

"Yes, that's just what it's like."

And when he was told to paste rabbit hair on his head so he'd look like a man again, and asked whether or not he was on pills all the time, he said:

"Yes—that's to be expected."

When he saw youngsters with glittering eyes after they drank, ready for mischief, he decided that that was so.

He put it down to determination.

When he heard that Cy had legal rights to the house he didn't question it.

When he heard that there were chemical sprays killing all the plants he said: "I imagine."

When he saw the prison he said:

"Yes—that's what we have."

When he thought of things then, he thought of everyone he had met, everything he had ever seen, every sign he'd ever read.

But he knew nothing about it.

Yet he would say:

"Randy would understand that."

Or, "My brother knew all about those things."

So people were at a loss to talk to him.

"If Randy were here he'd tell you a thing or two."

Or, "Randy didn't understand anybody any more than I did—"

Because Arnold looked the way he did, and upon reflection everything he did was done in an effort to improve his appearance, people had looks of mistrust on their faces when they saw him.

In his own heart he knew Craig to be a coward and a bully. This is what he knew in his heart.

But he never found out about his brother's last night, as he had about his mother. When he thought of his brother (he never thought of the face) he saw the tubular neck, and finely shaped head. He imagined him, with his knapsack open, handing candy about, and then running outside to get a bucket of water, and going along the cliff toward the path; and before reaching the path, falling 30 feet to the ice below, and smashing his head, and puncturing his kidneys.

This was what he thought about.

He thought about the finely shaped head and little tubular neck.

One day he took Randy's clothes to the dump and burnt them. The clothes Randy had had on when he went to the hospital, covered by spots of blood, and cut open by a nurse, were the last to be burnt. The sweater with the four badges Randy had sewn on with black thread—two on the chest and one on either arm—billowed and blew about in the heat. The heat grew noncommittal, a sudden sovereign in this arid pit, and he watched crows lift off the rusted hoods of death cars and lash themselves to the sky, much like burnt cinders.

Then he went home, and after listening to the hornets for ten minutes he got an idea of how to be rid of them.

He burnt the house to the ground.

Part Two

CHAPTER 1

I have lived here all the time. In the province of New Brunswick, Canada. From the beginning until now. The prison is here—do you know what they say? They say we won't get it. We have not gotten the helicopter base either but that's not news.

"Norman," they say, "you are a bad son of a bitch."

"Sure."

I nod neither one way nor the other for them.

When the priest came to my house, in the middle of the night, he spoke softly.

"Your wife has died," he said.

"Jenny—how?"

"Simply," he said. "In a car accident."

That was a bad time for me. I had just started back to night-school and was anxious about things. I sat at the back of the class that next evening and thought of Jenny.

Those things are said—that I didn't care for her. Well, I'll not answer to those things. It's like saying Seaweed didn't care for his mother or brother because he wouldn't go to the graves—and now he doesn't have to.

So when I think of Seaweed I think of the day they died. We went with him to town, to collect things, and took a taxi home. I'm not much good at saying anything.

"Why don't you come to live with me," I said.

But my girlfriend nudged me—because she didn't like the look of him.

"What if I end up having to do his laundry and picking up after him?"

So I don't blame her.

He was small and none of his clothes fitted him. I saw him at the circus after that.

He wanted an eagle tattooed on his bald head. The man said he wouldn't tattoo any man who was drunk and that was it.

Don't think I'm proud of everything.

I went to Jerry's one night after he'd beaten Arnold.

144

Trenda had the place smelling pink and filthy—there was too much heat in the rooms, too many odours and ideas hanging in the air. There was the heavy scent of macaroni in the kitchen, as if it had burnt the bottom of a pot, boiled away in the evening. It is bad to come upon a man when he is taking a bath. Who is the less at ease— who knows less how to treat the other, or how to get along? His white body, cast upon the enamel, the faucet still dripping, monotonous as torture, and the girl's shaven leg hair swept into the corner, under my feet, made me at odds with myself.

Jerry looked at me. He smiled all the while, and I could see his black eyes clearly.

"Touch him anymore and that's it," I said.

So I thought it would be over.

This road tells you everything. It only takes time to sink in. It is like everywhere else.

Shortly after this, Jerry was questioned about the vault again. He had been questioned so long he felt he'd no other choice but to sell some things he'd stolen and get away. Perhaps this was a stupid thing. I don't know about it, one way or the other. It was all cheap jewellery except for two diamond rings.

Trenda said she didn't know Jerry had stolen it. But no-one believed her. She even wore it to town the day she attempted to sell it.

She appeared in court. The windows were filled with beams of light. Mr. Matheson ran from the back benches and spit at her for desecrating his wife's coffin, but he was hustled away, and after the commotion all was still again. She didn't wipe the spit away but let it trickle down the side of her face, over her pink makeup. The judge ordered her to wipe it off and then ordered her counsel to wipe if off for her.

She sat there, staring quietly ahead, quite beautiful. The beams of light shone on the thousands of papers and long worn benches of a place I can truthfully say I dislike.

She looked very much her own woman.

Jerry was tried separately, and brought in shackled.

He yawned and looked about.

Everyone said we were rid of them.

Everyone said we were rid of them, and could breathe a little freer.

The Norwegian's picture still hung in our post office though—a picture of a man, no older than 26, with fine, pleasant features, that no-one really believes was murdered in the first place.

So I went home. I sat in the house and studied.

If I tell you I was disgusted all last winter I tell you the truth. I knew that Randy tried to lift weights to help him get strong. He did this so Craig would like him. Yet when I told this to Arnold he said:

"I know—so what—Craig is right."

"Craig doesn't know how to treat people."

"Maybe he does, maybe he doesn't—I don't want to talk about it."

But that's all I could get out of him.

We sat in the snowy field at supper hour, on a night the deer were running. There was a moon as splendid as this road has ever created, lying above us, and far away, down over the hill, the houses, with smoke coming up from their various dark bottoms. Christmas was over, finished; and I knew how he'd planned to have a good Christmas for them.

Ahhh.

It was a good night to talk to him.

He kept covering his boots over with snow. He told me what he had gone to the police station about, and that the police were questioning him, and sooner or later he would talk—say anything, just for fun.

"Yes," he said, "some night I'll say something just for the fun of it."

I didn't know what he meant. So I said nothing for a long time.

He told me about Trenda, and that when she was a girl those things happened to her. Sometimes people tell you things everyone else already knows, as if they're a revelation. That's when you have a burnt taste in your mouth, and try to look straight ahead.

He told me he had run out of oil, and had no idea how to get it without Juliet there to help them.

I was angry with him.

Look I said, in winter they won't cut off your oil, just go to a telephone and call someone.

Who do I call?

Anyone.

Who's anyone?

An oil company!

He told me people shouldn't bother him as much.

This went on, until he went home, and I never spoke to him again about it.

Don't think I'm proud of everything.

For I should have had courage a long time ago. Instead I waited in my house, away from the world, and took no interest in the plight of my cousins. Everything that happened through the winter I knew about and sometimes I'd spend days looking at the snow—snow so sweet it would blind you, and send you running.

Some nights, when things were as bad as they were going to get at their house, Randy would come to my place for supper. Those were the best times I had. I'd make fishcakes and tea, and pudding for dessert, and we'd sit at the table—the very one I'd broken with my fist the night Jenny left me.

"How are things at the house?"

"Fine."

"How is Mabel?"

"Good."

"Is she still watching soap-operas?"

"Yes."

"Where did you get that cut on your cheek?"

"I slipped on the ice."

So the conversation would continue.

"How do you like Juliet?"

He wouldn't answer. He'd simply stare at me with those eyes. Eyes that could damn you with their budding hatred.

"How can Mabel watch her soap-operas now that Seaweed has broken the TV?"

"Don't blame Arnold—I broke it."

"You broke it?"

"Of course—I broke it—with my bad fist—"

He showed me his fist, hidden in his sweater, caked with dirt. It was quite funny.

"I'm getting to have a bad fist," he said.

Craig told him he was a weakling, and he was lifting weights in order to improve himself.

I told him not to worry about such nonsense.

"What does Craig make you do?" I said.

"Run laps."

"How many?"

"Fifty laps."

He stared at me. Tattoos burnt on my arms and my legs were aggravated.

"After you've run your laps what do you do?"

"Throw up."

"What does Craig say?"

"Nothing."

"Why?"

"He doesn't pay attention to me."

He told me other things—mostly in monosyllables, the way we all talk here. Our most poignant conversations being nothing but a word or two—not much more than that.

Mabel is getting a new coat.

Yes.

She saw it in the catalogue.

Yes.

And she has promised herself one since Remembrance Day.

What does Juliet tell you?

We must live as a family unit.

How would that be?

Like the foster home.

How do you like Juliet?

He wouldn't answer.

Some nights I would prepare supper and wait for him, but he wouldn't be along. He would have stayed after school to lift weights.

I would drink a beer.

I would ask questions and the road would answer.

The wind would come against the house like a blast of laughter.

There was nothing to explain to Arnold, for he knew the same things I did. He and I were both born here and have made the best of it.

This road is 100 miles, broken through the trees, between our small town and the American border. It cuts right across the back end of our province from north to south. So nights are long.

I've been agitated about how long the nights are. It makes my legs ache. Trenda isn't an easy girl to forget.

At first I was very coarse with her.

"What do you want?"

"Anything you do."

"How do you know?"

"Try me and find out."

"You might regret it."

"I doubt that—"

"Where's Arnold?"

"At the doctor's office with his mother—he'll be there all day."

"Go to hell."

She laughed.

I picked up a branch and struck her across her bare legs.

Ahh.

"You beat your wife too didn't you?"

"That's what they say."

"So now—you're all alone—"

Later that evening she came to my house, walking up from the beach. I sat in the living-room, pretending I had no idea why she had come. She smelled of thick perfume and her odour carried across the room.

Give me a towel.

Why?

I want to cover myself.

Do you?

I want to take off my sweaty clothes and dry my body.

Body?

That's what it is—my clothes are sticking to it.

I might have put an end to it there, but I gave her a towel and she covered herself and stripped her clothes away, leaving them in front of me on the floor.

She sat in the chair across from me.

What are you looking at?

You'd better leave!

What are you looking at?

She laughed, and called me Norman with the tip of her tongue, as if she were biting my name in two.

Such a crazy laugh. A laugh that showed that she had no use for herself. Enough to make me forget who she was.

Then there was the pregnancy and it fell like a rock onto the dull greed I had for her, and hit me across the head so that I bled from it.

The greed had disappeared from her by then. But not from me. I sat up nights waiting for her to come, praying that she would—yet when she did I was angry.

Why don't you dress properly?

Go to hell!

It's a simple request.

Shut up.

Why not put on some panties?

Go to hell!

You're a bitch.

You made me one.

Only me?

Others also—so what?

So there was nothing more to be said.

"Juliet wants to become my friend," she told me one night.

"Why?"

"She thinks I'm special."

"You are."

"She thinks I am—she tells me I have a good grasp of how women have suffered."

"What did you tell her?"

"I told her she is a coward, and if she didn't leave me alone I would kiss her on the mouth."

Her face was quite plain now that I think of it. With as much quantity of brooding dissatisfaction as I've ever seen. She'd been on her own since she was a child, wearing the jaunty clothes of adolescence—all our clothes manufactured in another country—and her eyes would sparkle when some mischief was afoot. Her eyes shone suddenly, and complete as if she didn't care for her own safety. When she laughed, her voice was gutsy, beautiful, like her eyes.

She had cursed me because I wouldn't marry her.

How could I?

For there was Arnold.

"Sometimes I'm envious—but mostly I am numb," is what Arnold said to me.

In the summer, Johnson's barn was once again turned to a profit, and boys and girls of all ages went there to play music. Seaweed, older than the others, was always with them, avoided as much as possible.

People said he wasn't mean.

Though he seemed crazy.

Though I don't know what he was one way or the other. Long ago I'd stopped trying to reason with him about things.

He went to see lawyers in town. He wanted money.

Why do you want money?

Because you have killed Randy.

They didn't know what he was talking about and he became a bother sitting in their waiting-rooms, with an army jacket with a homemade swastika etched above the pocket.

"Coming to see you is like going to a dentist," he told them, "because it's like getting teeth pulled to get you to listen to me—"

And he no longer had a tooth in his head.

He went back to the hospital, and began asking the nurse out. The teeth were carried about in his pocket, and he wore a red kerchief about his shiny neck, right around his windpipe. His head was shaven and oily. In the summer, on the hot days, he took his army jacket off and wore a cut-off black leather vest, which his frail arms protruded from. His tattoos, one between his shoulder-blades and the other of his nickname scratched across his arm, seemed to say a lot about him.

The nurse tried to avoid him.

When his mother and brother were in the hospital he had repulsed the other nurses on her floor. Only she had taken his hand and had talked to him. She had seen how he'd tried to cope with this. He had tried to be polite and not get into arguments. But soon he was talking in a loud voice—telling Sadie to shut her mouth, and threatening Harry.

When he came to her in the summer with his head shaven he repulsed even her.

"What are you going to do?" she asked him.

"Nothing!"

"I was thinking that you should do something to get out of your rut."

"We're all in a rut."

"Yes."

"Yes."

He hung about the hospital in the dreary parking-lot that smelled of cars banished from their factories. Birds that were hot and sullied in their feathers took moisture from the dry ditches.

And every second or third day, rain.

I don't know if he held a knife on the doctor when he went to the office.

I think that was made up.

Some youngsters beat him. But it seems to me Arnold took this wound and wore it well, right on top of his head, as the road was being obliterated in front of his eyes and changing his life. Though I think you can't change people by changing roads.

He liked Helix and other heavy-metal bands this summer and seemed to thrive on them. His eyes would light up when he heard murder in a song.

There is murder in all our songs now.

Murder in every note.

There was dissension in their house again. It rose like the black grass under the cot with the broken television sitting on it, rose across the road and down to the water. Rose like the cliff they had dug, so their house tettered on its blind stilts in the rainy summer days.

A summer with too much rain and the turnips drowning.

The potatoes turned black in the soil.

The hornets screaming against the inside of their windows, and broken voices coming from near the hallway, in the back porch.

"Why isn't Juliet here?"

"Why doesn't she help us—?"

They talked about Juliet and her short-sighted eyes, saying that this was why she saw only what she wanted to. They asked each other where she was, and made up places for her to go.

Why didn't she come any longer?

They said they wouldn't hold their breath waiting.

And did what they thought was just—told jokes about her.

Seaweed scratched his face raw thinking of her, and yelled at nothing, because as he said, no-one deserved to be left alone.

Then they forgot about her, and her small hands, held up in a gesture of peace the night someone punched her, was the only thing he remembered. Her face was forgotten; at best, the way she walked through their rooms was a clouded memory.

The road tells us things.

Sadie brought it home, and placed it before him though no-one wanted him to find it out.

153

"Randy was a bully."

"Go to hell."

"He burnt a cub with a frying-pan."

"Go to hell."

"And the other cubs chased him outside and he fell over the cliff."

There was silence.

"I'm a woman who minds her business, but it serves him right."

"Shut up or maybe I'll get angry."

"You think Randy was a good boy; Randy was a bully. He burnt a cub with a frying-pan—banged him over the head. The little cub said, 'oh my head.'"

There was no answer.

"All because of a bag of candy."

"Leave me alone."

"Just because of that—sometimes it's good not to have people around."

Ahh.

"The kind that hit people on the head."

Their patience had ended and their truce was over.

Some days Arnold was seen sitting on the cot beside the television, just for peace. The rain came down and ran over his head, the field had gone soft, the hedges stilled, as if sleeping it away.

Other days he'd be seen sleeping on the porch, covered in a blanket, when the graders started their motors.

He'd not move. The men would shout out at him:

"Get up lazy arse," they'd shout—making jokes we're all familiar with.

Some days he'd spend the whole afternoon fishing near the sewer pipe, with a worm.

It rained and the black spruce were angry, the gravel turned against the wind and the windows of houses were grey and weatherbeaten.

Plastic surrounded many of the houses.

Because they were taking the walls down.

To replace the insulation.

But who could make a picnic in the rain?

154

As far as the fire goes, who knows about it?

It happened during the dry stretch we had the last two weeks of July.

The house was ablaze before anyone knew about it, and its ashes and boards fell or blew onto the road below. The smell of it scattered like crumbs throughout our whole area, and we could taste it for days after—as a reminder.

A heat had come that drew salt from the flesh. The sky was pale blue, and crows looked like battered legions in the sky.

We know that Sadie—holding on to a few belongings—ran from the house yelling that he tried to burn her alive.

This was a terrible thing.

And Harry did not make it from the house at all—but succumbed on his cot in the bedroom upstairs, sleeping with his shoes on, pointed straight up like little beacons.

And Cy, who had paid the back taxes so he could own the place (and sell it to the government who were widening the road) had his wish without bothering to trouble the family.

And the Christmas tree that had been thrown into the yard sometime before, burnt like the burning bush.

Who knows if Seaweed tried to kill anyone? For my idea is not the judge's.

If only Sadie had said nothing about Arnold threatening them with a knife the night he kicked the television. But she ran from the burning building, her hair singed, and her ears smoking.

"Ahh—he's done it—done it after all," she said. Smoke came first out of her left ear, and then out of her right, as she said it.

Her tears, half for her son, and half in triumph, made her look mean; at the time we had the most sorrow for her.

Arnold said nothing.

For a long time.

He seemed amazed that everything was gone except a

few things that lay about the yard.

The only thing he managed to say was that the hornets had bitten him, and this vexed him.

He was vexed (this is the word he used).

"I was vexed."

The crown prosecutor said, "You were vexed."

This made us laugh.

Ridiculous, with his small body, his shaven oily head, his cut-off leather vest that showed his arm tattoo and his leather pants, with a silver chain for a belt, he could do nothing more than smile when I did. And his blinking and refusal to look into people's eyes, as always, made him look guilty.

At one point he sneered at everyone.

And at another, the leaden expression came over him, an expression that looks like a cold twilight October day —and can set one cold.

This expression helped him not at all.

It was the one he'd tried to assume in the hospital after his brother died, but never managed to. It is the expression closest to my heart.

The knowledge of it makes people leave you to yourself.

Arnold tried to explain living in his house of hornets. He took the time to explain how they went running amuck throughout his bedroom the evening he'd come home from burning his brother's clothes. They sat about anywhere they wanted, and built a nest in the dresser that summer.

He lit a broom ablaze and chased them in the dark.

And everything went crazy. The whining smell of hornets in their egg-like bodies.

But who could understand him.

Sadie, however, made a different impression. She told the court everything she could think of about her relationship with the family—how she tried to leave the house one night, but Arnold prevented her from doing so—how Randy was beaten blue by his brother and how Mabel was laughed at when she was sick—how Trenda was turned bad by this relationship, and how the baby wasn't even Arnold's; but mine.

Did she have to tell everything the way she had? Such are the laws of right and wrong—one supposes this is what will always happen as soon as someone gets the upper hand.

When she mentioned that the child wasn't his after all she waved her hand in the air—her skinny bonelike fingers in the autumnal afternoon, the straight grey-streaked hair, cut off jaggedly about her ears, her earring globular and tinted winerose.

Arnold's head trembled, like a small earthquake had taken place inside it. I sat four or five rows behind him, with my hands placed under my thighs.

I waited for him to turn around and look at me.

Sometimes houses are better burnt to the ground, and sorrow burnt away in the dirty air.

For a while, a night and a day, I thought—even prayed a little—that the judge would let him go, considering all he'd been through.

The judge, however, was lenient. And Arnold received two years less a day—which meant he didn't have to serve his time in the federal penitentiary, but at the provincial jail.

This was both good and bad, and I can understand better now how the judge decided fair punishment.

I couldn't understand it then. I wanted Arnold to look at me—but I don't know what I might have done if he had.

Father Billy told me, about this time, that he wanted to call a snake a snake, a spade a spade, a lie a lie and all the rest of it. What he wasn't prepared to do, was forgive himself for his inertia.

This is what he said to me, close to that day:

"I can't forgive myself for my blasted inertia!"

The way he pronounced the word blasted—a word we don't hear anymore—stunned me. It was like a soul had left the body and scattered into the atmosphere.

Another night, close to that day, Father Billy told me:

"Meddling has killed them—legislation has destroyed their house—how can anyone be legislated to have honour, to love or hope for goodness—when there is triumph in the social worker's face and pride in the scoutmaster's eyes?"

And so he worried about this, in his own private way, and got very drunk—three weeks in a row.

And bawled everyone out in church.

And mentioned things he shouldn't have mentioned in his sermons.

Rain returned to the roads. Swallows lay in the dark wet grasses. Old barn-boards blew down in the autumn wind.

I will say I thought of Jenny—it must have been the very hour she died, for it was that time of night. I awoke and thought of her, her pumpkin-coloured hair and rusty cheeks. The dress she wore, which had the hem hanging. I thought of all of this, and yearned to ask her something in my sleeping state.

What could I ask her, of her pumpkin-coloured head I think only of goodness?

And then the priest came and knocked on my door.

I did not tell him I was thinking of her—that she came to me in a dream and woke me up; for what would he think of me then? People sometimes take the truth as lies, in a demented way.

"Norman you are a bad son of a bitch."

I have learned to nod neither one way nor the other for them.

CHAPTER 2

The provincial jail is even farther away from anything than our houses are. Its cement bricks are washed white by the snow all the raw winter long, and in the summer it sits naked on a flat miserable acre of ground. The prisoners have more freedom here than they could ever imagine having in the federal penitentiary, and their slouching bodies are seen in the yard.

Two primitive wires run power into it, and a primitive telephone line runs out.

Its windows, covered in neat mesh, are eight feet tall and two feet wide.

There are baseball games in the summer.

And rock music in the cells.

Though things might be tranquil there and running its course—there are also rules.

I have seen the building in November with the silty smoke hanging over it, and it made me think and I will tell you—that we are all primitive in our dealings with everything. The woods surround it—but only on the horizon. It is a flat bare place dissected by little yellow roads that are frost-worn.

I am getting not to like things anymore. I am getting to argue with people more and more over things. My back gets hot and my eyes grow cold, my face as set as granite. They can look at me for an hour and I won't change my expression.

My girlfriend offers me books as some people offer others cups and saucers, pictures of the Queen on a horse or an axe to split wood.

She takes me to her family's house—its living-room is bigger than my house altogether—and I try to be polite. I hide my tattoos as best I can—but this is what I think. Though my girlfriend tells me I have grown up rough, she likes my tattoos.

She tells them how I'm finishing school.

And plan to go to university.

Her mother nods.

Her father smiles.

I sit for an hour in a chair, bolt upright in front of them.

My girlfriend smiles at everyone, as if to encourage us, and though I admire her a great deal I believe she has set her heart too heavy on the future.

When her father talks, I try to hold my tongue.

I know what he thinks of me, and he is right. I haven't been a part of anything before, and have no notion how to be a part of things now.

That might be true in a way. Though I do not intend to lose my discipline.

When we leave the house and walk up the snowy streets through this Christmas time, with the wind as fresh as beer, we have arguments over how I've acted.

"You weren't very talkative."

"No."

"You didn't go halfway to be friendly—you'll find that they are very ordinary nice people."

"Of course."

"You don't seem to be too happy with them."

"I've never seen so much food cooked so well—and so many cookies in the cupboards."

"Does this anger you?"

I must tell someone that she is always asking me questions like this.

For Christmas she bought me a heavy white pullover —but I've already worn it a little too much.

I've worn it three days in a row to their house.

I've worn it about too much. At first it felt as fresh as a new sprouted whisker—joyful with life.

"Why should food anger me?" I ask.

Food has never angered me before.

My short curly head of hair is quite beautiful on me, it is the most beautiful thing I have. I like it when she touches it with her gloved fingers in a night of gentle snow, and shining Christmas lights, and the bells of different churches pealing away softly in the distance.

When she gives me a book I stuff it away somewhere, and forget to look at it.

I spend just as much time alone as I always have. I don't mix well with people—that's been said often enough. I stare at the buildings an awful lot, and wonder why anyone built them. They seem disordered, cruel. There are always reminders of blood on the bricks, and unsatisfied calendars of years that have passed away.

Jenny was born in 1963.

She wasn't even twenty.

She always tried to wear skirts that would show her beautiful legs, even if she had to freeze in them in February. No-one here knows how to dress for winter even though they've spent their entire lives in it. The girls try to dress like some picture postcard of somewhere else, some city they've seen on television or in the movies.

And once, she got away to St. John, the largest city in our province, and came back with a present for all of us —that's probably the only place she got to.

I have bad dreams.

Always when I least expect them.

Of things I cannot understand.

Though perhaps schooling will take care of it.

I know Randy no longer feared anyone when he shoved an iron into his enemy's face.

The dream I have, whether asleep or awake, is the same.

When Arnold went to jail his hair started to grow out and sprouted like toothpicks over his head. Red hair stuck out of his scalp like tiny red carrots. And no-one can say that he wasn't in a strange world—the world of jail. His tattoos didn't match up to the tattoos that were there.

He spoke to no-one, so why should anyone speak to him? He did no-one favours, so why should anyone do any favours for him? Perhaps this was his plan. Perhaps this was what he finally thought of as determination. I have come to no conclusions about how he finally thought.

I was busy then—it was October, and I didn't get to see him.

I was working on my own plans.

So that's what I was doing. I was going to school in the evenings. And then I had to go to Jenny's funeral.

It wasn't a good time for me.

Though I don't make excuses.

The first night was a bad night, for him.

He pulled the blanket over him and tried to sleep. But he was disturbed by the person in the next cell.

"In here," the person in the next cell said, "you won't live long."

"Leave me alone—" Arnold said.

The next day Arnold sat in his cell, smoking cigarettes.

"Go out for exercise," Monroe, the jailer said.

"I think I'll stay here and be as pleasant as I can—and cause no-one problems," Arnold said politely.

But he was put outside like a child dressed in a snowsuit. He stood against the wall, watching a game of touch football in the gathering dark. The gloomy smell of October had touched the leaves, and the scent of codfish gave him the dark lonely feeling all over again. He looked at the sky and saw an American jet crossing it. Just before dark, they were herded in again. There were twelve prisoners. Not many, and he heard a bird sing, feather-worn, in the windy grass.

The second night was a bad night. Toffy, a short little man, strong as a pitbull, who'd run his brother's car off a wharf for the insurance, sneered at him, spitting on the floor when Arnold passed by.

"Cunt," Toffy said.

He went back to his cell. Even when they locked it, it didn't stop his heartbeat. His heartbeat bothered him all night long, tucked up as he was, smelling his own body.

"You'll get yours," came the voice from the next cell.

Arnold gathered all his courage, like he had the night he followed Trenda to town, just a year ago. A year that wasn't entirely prosperous.

"Hey you," he said.

No-one answered.

"Can't you leave me be—I'm just recovering from a tragedy."

There was no answer.

The first week, he saw a line on his floor drawn by a previous prisoner. It was a line a foot away from the cell bars. He decided not to cross it to go out of his cell, and to ask for his meals inside.

"You do what the others do," Monroe said.

Arnold sat on his cot.

"I don't have a hair on my body," he said.

He wanted Monroe's sympathy.

But there was no answer.

Sometimes he would talk to himself about Pacman and Outriders. But no-one was interested. And when anyone wanted a cigarette they invaded his package. But after they did this they said nothing to him.

"Snitch," Toffy said.

Arnold looked away, as if he were being hit.

He had one visitor in this time.

It was the nurse.

"I'm going to take the transcript to a board of inquiry," she told him.

He looked at her. Red hair stuck out of his scalp like tiny red carrots, except for the middle strip, which was darker and more matty.

He shrugged neither one way nor the other.

"I'm going to resign," the nurse told him. "So I've nothing to lose by doing this—it isn't a favour. The doctor made four serious misjudgments."

"Misjudgments," Arnold whispered hoarsely. He had a cold again. And things were dizzy.

"Misjudgments," the nurse said. "He left her dying of infection—"

Arnold said nothing. He asked the nurse for a cigarette, for every day they stole his package, and when she gave him one he puffed away on it solemnly.

"Misjudgments," he said, "yes, misjudgments." He sniffed the smoke like a dog finding an old familiar scent. Even though the cigarette was menthol.

"It doesn't matter," he said. "She's better off."

He noticed the wedding ring on her finger, and smiled. His eyes were wide and the whites of them were yellow.

The nurse got nowhere with her board of inquiry, as it

turned out.

It was November. Frost blanched the ground and hardened the footprints.

When Toffy saw him later that day, sitting in his cell with the door open, smoking a menthol cigarette he saw something innocent and indulgent about the way Arnold inhaled, and stabbed him with a wooden knife. It caused a good deal of bleeding, but no-one mentioned it.

Arnold resumed talking to himself. About Pacman. He knew all the tricks when it came to playing Star-Invaders and talked to himself on that topic also.

I know for a fact that he did this. It was told to me.

Again he was worried about the hair on his body, because he used a common shower, the gunnels of which had gone to rust, the smell of human odour.

"A hairless man is his own worst enemy—I'm quite sorry I never grew."

After he was stabbed with the wooden knife, the rest of the men had no use for him.

November was dry and sour-looking, crazy with wind and dancing snow, and ice curdling the trunks of poplar shoots.

After Toffy had stabbed him he made himself a wooden knife but his heart wasn't in it. He no longer had the determination to stab anyone. He knew Jerry Bines had put Toffy up to it. Jerry Bines seemed to pit the other prisoners against each other whenever he wanted.

It wasn't long before Seaweed was counting the snowflakes as seconds going by. Though by now everyone had heard of Mabel and Randy. And Jerry Bines forced his opinions on everyone.

"Randy was a worthless tub of shit."

"Mabel was a worthless cunt."

He heard that all night long.

"When are you going to let me out of my cell?" Jerry Bines said.

"Don't worry about it," Monroe said.

Jerry sat in his cell, his thick ankles covered by oppressive-looking socks. His forehead was white with scar tissue.

"Jerry Bines, you're just a road-hugging machine," Seaweed said.

There was no answer.

Toffy was the feet for Jerry Bines. He was the eyes for Jerry Bines. Those eyes watched Seaweed until the lights went out.

Seaweed sang commercial jingles one after the other. Though he liked Helix and other heavy-metal bands, the jingles were the only things he remembered.

It bothered people to hear him. He had a voice like his mother—he couldn't carry a tune, a voice that seemed to run out of him like water.

"You must let him out of his cell," Arnold said. He said that to every guard on duty. He began to say it day and night.

"You must let Jerry out of his cell—you can't keep a man caged like an animal."

"Why are you going to bat for me—you'd better not say anything on my account—" Jerry whispered.

Arnold talked to himself. He didn't sleep or eat for two days. He simply talked to himself. He asked Sadie to forgive him.

Then he continued: he continued in the exercise yard.

"You must let him out of his cell—you can't keep him caged in there—I'll go to the social services—you have to let him out."

"What's he talking about?"

And at night he continued.

"When I get out of this cell I'm going to kill you for lying about me," Jerry whispered. "I know who went to the cops!"

"When will you kill me?" Arnold whispered.

"When I get out of this cell," Jerry whispered.

There was a pause.

"You have to let him out of his cell—it isn't humane to keep a person locked away without exercise—if you can't control him here then you should send him somewhere else—you have to let him out of his cell."

"Shut up," Jerry said.

The police did no favours for Jerry Bines, and he did no favours for them. It started long ago with the police. They did no favours for him, for a long time. When he went to jail—he received the same sentence as Arnold, two years less a day—they knew he was a bad apple. They knew that from day one, and treated him accordingly. One day led to the next and soon he was being locked up during exercise. Soon he was let out of his cell only to shower.

Everyone who went to jail knew that Jerry Bines was there also.

Who is up there?

Jerry Bines.

So they knew who they would have to deal with.

I think Arnold sat alone, like a sad bird, watching the snow.

I don't think he went to confession before he died.

I think people like to make up stories.

And some people say he fought like a wild animal and tore his cell apart.

I have sat with his death a month on my shoulders.

When I go to Nancy's father, he says what I've heard before.

He sits at the table and looks at me. He is a businessman selling warehouse furniture in the backend of nowhere.

He reminds me of a man being dusted off by a barber.

That is all I can say for him.

"Didn't they hit the guard over the head?"

This is all he says. I know he'd like a bad reaction—something that would prove to him what he thinks. Suspicions like that always crop up whenever I talk to anyone.

(I know for a fact no-one was hit over the head. It's just something people who are so careless say, on a public holiday.)

I know they ran into the woods.

Jerry and Toffy, when they pried apart the wire over the shower window.

Arnold ran right behind them when he saw his chance to go.

It was the silliest thing he ever did. But his life was filled with ideas that didn't come together.

I have asked the nurse.

I have asked Father Billy.

I have asked Nancy.

They say:

"How can you tell what he was up to?"

If I had known they were only two miles from here, in Jerry's grandmother's barn I might have acted differently.

But I had no reason to know.

Jerry had only his underwear about him, and Arnold took off his clothes and gave them to him.

He sat alone and covered his stomach with wet hay.

And he wouldn't stop talking.

"Stop him from talking," Toffy said. "He's driving me nuts."

Jerry pulled on Arnold's pants and shirt, which he took as his right, and smoothed his hair back with his hands. Arnold had a sprout of hair here and there on his head. He had no more hair on his body.

They were waiting for Trenda. Trenda who had by then left us all behind.

"When Trenda comes things will be different," Arnold kept saying.

He kept saying this.

"When Trenda comes everything will be better."

Jerry told him to shut up.

And Arnold had two tattoos. One of a cross that ripped across his back, and one of his nickname stencilled on his arm. It was a ludicrous thing. His tattoos weren't much compared to theirs.

"Trenda will come," Arnold said. "God bless Trenda."

"They know where we've headed—by our footprints—"

Jerry's feet were cut and bled on the snow.

"It's almost dark—"

"Tell him to shut up—"

"Someday I'm going to have a house like Matheson's —with a duck pond."

"Tell him to shut up."

"That's one thing I always wanted, a duck pond."

Arnold sniffed and scratched his nose. He took his time scratching it, and came to some conclusions.

"Then I'd fill it with ducks—and hunt them, from my bedroom."

Arnold calmly gave Jerry his shoes and socks. Nothing fitted properly—everything was too small. Jerry complained about this and seemed aggravated.

Snow came in through the cracks in the walls, and boards moaned in the wind. The night was clean, and hardened with stars. There was no area as hard, no stubble as black or as painful to naked feet.

"I'm quite cold," Arnold said.

He said that only once.

He told them about Stephen who couldn't stand the cold, and wondered where he was.

"By morning they'll know where we are," Toffy complained.

Trenda didn't come.

"When Trenda gets here everything will be better," Arnold said. He sat twenty feet away, and they let him no closer.

No-one answered. Everyone was too cold. And after a while Jerry and Toffy lit a fire, and stood with their backs to him.

Arnold smiled.

Jerry said something.

And everyone nodded. Arnold nodded when Toffy did. He wanted to nod the same way.

"Snow will cover our tracks," Jerry said.

For a long time they were silent, watching the fire go out.

Now and then Arnold lightly touched his head with dignified gestures.

Others say he put up a fight against them to stand

168

beside the fire.

Jerry is the one alone.

And other prisoners remember things a long time.

I have seen the hole they'd busted in the window as if it had been busted out with sudden impact. I've seen the footprints too—not many of them. I have seen a little blood.

Do you know what I think?

There is always something vulgar in men running away.

The trees are stark in there. The bog is frozen. The last days of the year glimmer and brush the ground in a dying stroke. The coyotes have come.

They have come in packs, and roam the shale hillsides.

So I went to Trenda. By her own good fortune she never served a day in jail.

She stared at me when I asked her those questions.

Truly she has her apartment decorated in bad taste.

"I didn't know anything about it."

"Then why were they waiting all night for you—?"

She smiled slightly, and shrugged. She is living with a man of 40 with grey hair on his belly. They too want to have a Christmas. They have a string of red lights over their window, and a manger sitting on woollen snow.

When I came close enough I smelled her hot breath in my face, and her cheeks, flushed from the flu, smelled of blood. Her hair was knotted in curious passions. Her ears, freshly pierced, were clean and catlike resting against her skull. Her skull shadowed the wall. The light of the bakery across the street flashed once and twice against her open legs.

So I don't know what to think.

Jerry says he will kill her.

And I'm certain she knows it.

There'll be many long nights of waiting.

"I think you love her a little," my girlfriend says.

She says that often enough—but she shouldn't tease me.

The prison rises. It keeps its face well hidden.

The new road they are building cuts right across the remains of Arnold's house. An old cot with a broken television remains to be bulldozed away, and the snow has come and has made it harsh and quiet there.

The Norwegian might have been killed a dozen ways. Or he might never have been hurt at all. No-one knows about him anyway, and after a while his picture was taken down.

Jerry and Toffy were caught running back toward the jail. They deserted each other at the last, and each tried to get away by himself. Jerry can fight, he has fought all his life against them, but Toffy gave up. Now one accuses the other of my cousin's death, and neither of them are apt to do the other favours. I too will wait, for a long time if I have to.

Who knows what the police are thinking.

The police can think what they will about someone wearing someone else's clothes.

My girlfriend is pretty, a small thing, with ideas of her own. I tell you I think this, when I visit Jenny's grave. A grave without a marker but I intend to buy one for it.

My girlfriend tells me how to act and I try to act that way. When we have money we share it, and we've opened a bank account. I think I've made too much of this bank account—for I carry my account book everywhere with me, and keep it in my pocket.

I am very happy with this Christmas eve. I have never seen snow come so serenely to the ground. Or a tree with such decorations.

Billy the priest is an alcoholic.

The nurse thinks it's her fault for not pressing with the inquiry into the death of his mother. It never went anywhere because she got frightened of the weight that might come down on her.

Sadie has moved into the senior citizen's home. Her wit is sharper than anyone else's, and no-one takes advantage of her.

Who dragged Arnold's naked body 30 yards?

This is what some of us want to know.

The road, sooner or later, will tell us everything. We only have to wait.

A little Christmas music plays so tenderly that Nancy's brother keeps filling my glass with red wine.